When My Sister Was Cleopatra Moon

When My Sister Was Cleopatra Moon

Frances Park

talk miramax books
HYPERION
NEW YORK

Library of Congress Cataloging-in-Publication Data

Park, Frances, 1955-
   When my sister was Cleopatra Moon: a novel/by Frances Park.—1st ed.
   p.cm.
   ISBN 0-7868-6647-0
   1. Korean American families—Virginia—Fiction. 2. Korean
Americans—Virginia—Fiction. 3. Korean American women—Fiction. 4.
Sisters—Virginia—Fiction. I. Title.
PS3566.A6732 W48 2000
813'.54—dc21   99-054524

First edition

Book design by Lovedog Studio

10 9 8 7 6 5 4 3 2 1

To my dad, who lives on. . .

Acknowledgments

GRATITUDE goes to my brilliant editor, Jonathan Burnham, who flew down twice to talk with me about the manuscript—a class act. And to the miraculous Molly Friedrich, the agent of all get-out. Never to be forgotten: My best friend and baby-faced sister Ginger; my beautiful and hip mom; Walt for the giant chocolate aspirin; and Moondoggy (from your Gidget).

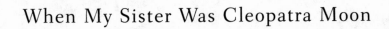

When My Sister Was Cleopatra Moon

MOMENTS AGO, on this evening of the day Cleo's husband was buried and after the last guest was gone, a summer thunderstorm struck without warning. Again. Lightning danced like ghosts on the bay and Cleo made her bewitching entrance while I rocked her younger child, June Moon, to sleep. At forty-two, the widow Cleo is still gorgeous. Impossibly so. Her lustrous black hair gives off pearls and those eyes could stun a dead man back to life. Well, almost. All day Cleo has wept crocodile tears with in-laws she despises more than ants in her sesame noodles. Now she's fixing up her own storm—a late supper for us—while the sympathy buffet goes cold. The delight she takes in stir-frying vegetables alarms me, as does the way she pours on something called Cha Cha Cha Chili Sauce with drunken abandon. After all, her husband is dead.

Behind a veil of smoke she grieves. "How will I fill my days without Stu?"

She's already doing it, spooning sizzling vegetables onto plates. Sauces, her *raison d'etre*. How can she cook at a time like this? Much less eat? Maybe the answer lies behind the smoke screen.

O N L Y I know the real Cleo. Her darkness. Others see a delicious Asian woman who bottles sauces with her picture on every label. But I see a girl who rode the rocky waves, then settled down with Stu, a rich guy by way of Brooklyn, then Wall Street, now Montgomery Street. He was older, possibly insecure. Did she love him? Could Cleo ever love a bald guy? Or anyone?

When she called me two days ago—her first call to me in years—it was to tell me that Stu was dead. According to Cleo, they were driving home from a dinner party when a thunderstorm struck out of nowhere. Stu was driving. A bolt of lightning blinded him, and he lost control of the car. They veered off the left-hand side of the road. That's all she remembers. After I expressed my shock and condolences, I asked Cleo whether she was hurt. "Oh, no, I'm fine" was her matter-of-fact reply.

I came face to face with Cleo's darkness a long time ago. But I'm not here to judge her today, despite what history breeds.

If I were home, none of this would be in my eyes or ears. I could trade in this spicy plate for a bowl of Pablo's soup and ponder desert peace. If I were home, the world would fall into place again. The wind would come through the house, bringing all the spirits with it. My bones would settle my soul down. If I were home, I'd chalk up my uneasiness to a bitter herb and make a pot of chamomile tea.

June Moon would like it there. I could rock her to sleep to the distant sounds of wild horses and our rivers to nowhere. And she would sleep as she's never slept. So soundly. The assault of radio, television, telephones would not creep into her dreams.

Think of a big city, then the opposite edge of the earth. Think of a million-dollar home, then of a cabin with floors that creak with secrets and worn curtains that speak for themselves. A porch out front, a second-story porch out back. Downstairs is our shop; upstairs is our home. Here, in between our dreams, Pablo and I make our life.

Cleo frowns. My bare-bones living makes no sense. No money. No man. Pablo doesn't count: he's blind in one eye—a freak. No plans to create a sauce a minute. How appalling. We don't shoot for the same stars. How could we be sisters?

Pablo and I like modest living; it grounds us to our purpose. We fix up a big pot of soup Sunday night and it lasts all week. The potatoes soak up the broth, and by Wednesday it's stew. To Cleo, it's the same old soup.

A candle burns between us in memory of Stu. No sad ceremony here. Cleo's face grows radiant. Between bites, she says, "So you're still at that thrift shop, what's it called?"

"Cactus Bear," I reply, "and it's not a thrift shop. I mean, we don't sell junk."

"But some of the things you sell are used." She shudders.

"Yes, but we like to call it hand-to-heart art."

"Do they pay you enough?"

"Actually, no one pays us. We work for food, shelter, and the knowledge that we're helping others."

"So what do you live on?"

"Soup."

She groans. "I honestly don't get it, Marcy. You could have been anything you wanted to be. What the hell happened? Why do you live on soup?"

"I love soup."

"Look, at least I can admit I was a drifter who was looking to land happiness and got lucky. But you, you were a phenom. You could juggle a dozen books at once. You aspired!"

I correct her. "You aspired for me."

She thoroughly doubts me. "Did I?"

ONCE WE were so close our flames burned as one. Now no more. Cleo put us out. Except for a few scattered letters and phone calls, she was not in touch for years. No wonder our touch today is cool. Yes, her husband is dead but I barely knew him, might not recognize him in a crowd. So why did she plead with me to come here? And why did I come?

THE HOUR is late, the thunderstorm is over. We're on a palatial balcony with a view of the Bay. Fog rises like ghosts in my eyes.

"Why did you want me to stay on, Cleo? You had four hundred guests at the funeral. Why did you say I had to stay or a quake would swallow you up whole?"

"Because something's wrong with Luke."

Luke is thirteen, father unknown. At the time Cleo was working as an exotic dancer.

"He's not sick, is he?" I ask.

"No, he's not sick. At least, not physically. See, Luke's a loner at heart, he always has been, but now he's brooding in cyberspace. He can't hear me up there and he won't come back down to earth."

"He just lost his stepfather, the only real dad he's ever known. I'm sure he's in a great deal of pain."

"Yes, I know that, but that's not it."

"How do you know that's not it?"

"This has been going on for a while," she explains. "Before Stu, it was always Luke and me. We were inseparable, we lived like gypsies. We went to the zoo, parades, fairs. When Stu came along, Luke took to him right away. Stu was thrilled, of course. He married late and fatherhood was never on his list of things to do. But he was good at it, like everything else. The two sailed, played golf, tennis. But a few months ago, Luke called it off, said he was too busy, which was bull considering he spends half his time playing Suicide Spell at some horrendous hangout called Pier Pressure with a bunch of average little shits. It's especially heartbreaking because Luke is like you, a high-IQ-er. Anyway, Stu was crushed, naturally, but he never let on. The problem is that Luke is so defensive. I try to talk to him, confront him, but he won't let me within arm's length anymore. My God, do you think my own son hates me?"

For all I know, the widow Cleo may be faking her tears for Stu. But this is Luke, her flesh and blood, the son she gave up her tassels for.

"Of course not," I say.

"Then what?"

"Maybe he's jealous of June Moon," I submit. "Her biological father was around and his wasn't."

"Nonsense. We've always been open on the subject of his mystery dad—that's what Luke calls him. Sometimes a man of a certain description—tall and blond with wire rims, don't ask me why—will pass us and Luke will look at me like *Is he the one?* So it's not like some twisted secret that's weirded him out."

"Then I give up. I'm sorry, Cleo. I wish I could help."

"Marcy, you can't give up just like that. You were always good with kids. You had those magic brain waves going," she says.

"I did?"

"Yes, yes, you brought those two backward brothers out of their fogs, remember?"

The memory glows in the back of my head. Two backward brothers. Out of their fogs. A tiny black poodle, shivering in the corner. *Come here, Afro, come here.* Such a helpless thing. A voice, ancient and haunting, whispers to me. *Cactus Bear, Cactus Bear, Cactus Bear.*

"You've got to help me, Marcy," Cleo's pleading.

Wasn't coming here enough? What got into me in the first place? Even though Pablo doesn't know the whole story, he told me to grow up and try to forget all the bad blood. When I told him I happen to still be bleeding, he rolled his good eye. So I walked out of Cactus Bear without a farewell meditation.

"The last nanny left without notice and I'm pulling my hair out over what to do. Marcy," she utters as if her life depends on it, "there's another reason I wanted you to stay."

"What is it? Tell me."

"I need your help while I prepare for and attend the Global

Gourmet Food Show next week. I need you to watch Luke and June Moon. Will you do it?"

"Cleo, I can't believe what I'm hearing. Your children have just been left fatherless. June Moon is barely ten months old. What could be so important about some food show?"

"It's not just some food show, Marcy. It's the big trade show where all the buyers in the food industry descend on New York to see what's new out there, what's hot. I did the San Francisco show last winter and nearly doubled my business. This one's even bigger. It's a market I haven't cracked yet. I've already booked a booth, but what with the funeral, I haven't had a chance to get my act together. The price sheets got lost and the publicity packets are still at the printers. I'm introducing six new sauces and the labels came in gold instead of copper. But I absolutely can't miss this show, Stu wouldn't want me to; it's been in the works for months now. Don't you see, it's my chance to expand Cleo's Creations outside the West Coast. It's my East Coast debut! I'll pay you double what you make, Marcy."

"I make nothing," I remind her.

"Okay, well, stay twelve days and I'll create a sauce in your name," she says. "A tempting offer, wouldn't you say? You can't pin a price on fame."

Cleo and I are not on the same globe; we spin in different directions. Her orbit is fame and million-dollar homes and sauces called Wild Oriental Plum and Mango Tango Glaze. From where she's spinning she can't see who I am.

Cactus Bear is who I am. Pablo and I opened Cactus Bear on a whim; we were in Nevada in a Bob's Big Boy, of all places, when we heard from a moccasin maker the legend of the White

Sky Indians. The ancient White Sky were magic—they could turn fires into stars and bones back into buffalo—but their magic put fright in the heart of other tribes. So they were banished to a plot of land in Nevada and they named it after themselves, White Sky.

At the time Pablo and I had just met and wanted to find a common ground to live. Somewhere with no memories, somewhere where we could make them. In White Sky we found it in the form of an abandoned trading post that would become Cactus Bear. Our rent is free and we pay no taxes, but that's the limit of federal help. And the state, forget it; no provisions. We're a ghost town, not on the map. Because the White Sky only number seven hundred and twenty at last count, they are a lost, forgotten, impoverished tribe. No leader comes forth. A group called Native Americans in Need organizes craft and nature events and creative education classes, but the White Sky desperately need a clinic. Not a medical clinic—there's one next door in Mesa Crossing—but an herbal healing clinic. If their souls don't get attention, their culture will die.

At Cactus Bear we sell White Sky artifacts, new and used. Pottery, moccasins, coiled baskets, pictorial rugs, beaded vests, the most magnificent decorated water jugs this side of the Great Basin desert. We're not a tourist spot but people seem to find us. Pablo says we're listed in some guide called Gault-Millau. We're not a trading post but we've been known to make a swap or two.

At Cactus Bear, all profits go to the White Sky. We're here to display their art, to help their ancestors rest in peace. We're here to make sure mouths are fed. But only an herbal healing clinic can help restore their magic. Otherwise, they'll suffer extinction.

At Cactus Bear, we operate under our own system. We set our own hours, lock up when the chimes just inside the door go still. There is no fear, no room for it in our lives. What I read in the *San Francisco Chronicle* does not compute in White Sky.

"Marcy?"

"Cleo, I'll help you if you help me."

"Name your price."

"Sponsor me for my Moccathon."

She laughs. "Your whatathon?"

"My Moccathon. It's a walkathon organized by Native Americans in Need. The money will go toward building an herbal healing clinic for the White Sky tribe. I've rounded up some sponsors but they're stingy state officials who just want my vote. It would mean a lot to me. And to the White Sky."

Her lower lip quivers. She's so amused. "I see."

"If you promise to pledge fifty dollars a mile, I'm yours for twelve days."

How many miles could I possibly walk, she's calculating. Five? Ten? Cleo can laugh and quiver all she wants. Her limited vision just might bankrupt her.

"Deal!" she says.

In the name of the White Sky tribe and Cleo's kids, I'm giving up my half-pot of soup and twelve days with Pablo. Twelve nights of meditation, of reaching Cactus Bear. Ever since his cooking class, he's taken over the stove. He says my batches are bland, I say his are heavy on the herbs.

·   ·   ·

THE BAY air drifts with jazz through twin windows in the bedroom. Pale, frilly curtains move like unsettled spirits. I smell rain, summer, a San Francisco night. I am not used to this smell or the feel of this room. I am already lonely for home, for my big lumpy bed. Surely this bed is brand new, for show only. The mattress is so hard every bone in my body aches. And the pristine sheets scratch me with every toss and turn. Surely no one has ever fallen into a deep dream here.

A bed should be worn down with dreams. But I will not dream tonight. Not because June Moon is crying in the background. I will not dream tonight because questions are crossing my mind like trains over tracks. Is Cleo a good mother? Was she a good wife? Was she a good sister?

2

CLEO WAS back, her red convertible Mustang was lined up with the buses. I remember running down the school steps so fast I beat the bell. When she saw me, she went wild with her signature honk—*beep, beep, beeeep!*—calling up something I can't imagine today. My big sister at the wheel. My heart racing.

"Cleo, you're home!"

She hugged me like a beloved rag doll and wouldn't let go for a long time. I needed that hug, it almost got me crying. What stopped me was the shocking sight of her bosom plunging out of a red-and-white-striped tube top. In those days I lived in Cleo's hand-me-downs—her faded jeans and old T-shirts—but the thought of me in that tube top next year was going too far. I would never have deep cleavage or wear Wet 'n' Wild hot pink lip gloss so deservedly. And my hair was black straw, no matter how I cut it. It would never move like the ocean when I walked.

Our mother often pointed out that Cleo inherited her beauty from our grandmother, but Cleo brushed this off like dirt. I don't think she wanted to be linked in any way to some Korean peasant squatting in the fields. Could I blame her?

Cleo played with the tuner on the radio, her wrist jingling with silver bangles. "I can't get over how *cute* you're getting, li'l one. I'm *so* jealous," she said, lying through her teeth. When she found her song, she lip-synched and her faux-diamond-studded sunglasses caught the sun in a dazzling display of how the whole world can miraculously turn cool. The top was down and the sky was blue. Cleo shifted into gear.

"Hang on, school's out for the summer!"

With one rebellious thrust we zoomed past Glover Intermediate and Bus 14. I secretly flipped off the creeps on the bus—namely, Mitch Mann, Dave Kelly, and Frog Fitzgerald. Next year they'd get me, at another school, on another bus—probably spend their whole stupid summer thinking up a new name to call me—but now I was with Cleo. Idol of my life and the hereafter. In this world, in this Mustang, they were nothing to me.

WE WERE on the Beltway, weaving between trucks. Our destination: Taco Town, two exits up. If Taco Town were a million miles up we could keep on driving. Watch the sun set and the moon rise in our eyes. If the exit ramp curved on forever, we could go round and round and round it like a carnival ride. I could do it, live on the edge of a spectacular never-ending dream: Cleo and me, running for our lives. It would beat real life, as long as it would last. It would beat reading *American*

Teen magazine, if I never woke up. When we got to Taco Town, we pulled into the drive-thru.

The summer before Cleo had a boyfriend named Leonard who worked here on weekends. He was older than Cleo, with a stringy blond ponytail, though his beard was reddish-brown. She dumped him, but she still hungered for Leonard Lewandowski's love, day and night.

"He really loved me, Marcy. He would shoot old ladies if I told him to. *Two beef 'n' bean burritos and two large Tabs!*" she hollered into the mike.

"He had a neat van," I said.

A cruel smirk came over her face, one I easily recognized. She was reliving the night she broke Leonard's heart, the night she cruised through the drive-thru with her hands all over Chuck Boucher. They'd been to a pool party and had drunk tequila under the deck. How many times had I heard the story?

We took our food and parked in our old spot, which faced a run-down route of strip shopping centers and whizzing traffic. It was bleak, for Washington, D.C., suburbia. Potholes, U.S.A. Namely, Glover, Virginia. And there we savagely ate that afternoon in 1976. Nothing ever tasted so good, as we wolfed down pillows of grease, the traffic music to my ears. In a blinding sun my eyes squinted into mere slits as Cleo lit up a menthol cigarette like a movie star.

"Are you home for the summer?" I asked her. "The whole summer?"

My loneliness always hit her right in the gut. She crumpled up the bag with conviction. "I'm not going anywhere, li'l one. You want to go to the mall, we go to the mall. You want to go to the pool, we go to the pool. Get the picture? It's you and me from now on. The rest of the world can go up in flames."

"You mean until September," I said.

"No, I mean from now on. I'm thinking about dropping out of Jamestown, a.k.a. Dumbo U," she said.

My heart stopped like a clock. Cleo and me, Cleo and me, Cleo and me. Just like the old days!

"But Mom and Dad will kill you!"

"I don't care! I can't face all those Petunias in the dorm again! Pigs!"

I knew all about them. I had read every one of her letters from college so many times I knew them by heart. There was Libby, who went around telling everyone Cleo was a syphilitic slut. And Patty, who claimed she saw her making out with a girl in some townie bar. And Maureen, who spread a rumor on frat row that Cleo shaved her breasts. An article in *American Teen* magazine—"Make Friends with Jealous Foes"—said to take the calm, rational approach. *Take a deep breath. Talk it out.* But Cleo could drive girls to murder. Their angry eyes were on her everywhere we went. In malls, at the movies. Everywhere!

Three guys walked by us, going nuts over Cleo like cars out of control.

Va-va-voom!

Give papa a kiss!

Sweet mama!

Cleo flashed them a smile that could make her famous. To me she *was* famous and I was content to live in her glamorous fog.

"Cleo, every guy on the face of the earth wants you," I moaned, knowing that's what she wanted to hear. The world moaning her name.

She basked in her glory with a marvelous sigh and a flip of her sunglasses. That's when I saw what I'd be staring at all summer. Her eyes! They were painted black with dramatic wings at the tips.

"Cleo?"

She winked. "Call me Cleopatra."

WE WERE called Cleo and Marcy, but those were not our birth names. We had adopted them at some point and thrown the others away as if to hide the evidence, even from ourselves. The occasional sight of Misook on my report card struck a nerve and for an ugly moment I was reminded of who I was. The only Oriental girl this side of the planet. Besides Cleo, of course. But she didn't count. Who on earth would make fun of her? She walked with her head up high, crowned by her own confidence.

Now she had those eyes! They came out of a tiny Max Factor bottle I had seen advertised in *American Teen*. It was labeled Waterproof Eyeliner, and they weren't kidding. Cleo slept and showered and swam in those eyes—they never came off. After a while I got used to them, although my parents didn't.

"You are not Cleopatra under this roof!" my father argued. He was a Harvard man, born to debate. But not with his daughters. "You are Kisook Moon. Do you understand? Do you hear me?"

"Don't call me that." She covered her ears. "I am Cleopatra Moon, I am Cleopatra Moon, I am Cleopatra Moon!"

My father had endured many hardships in his life, but none could affect him like the disobedient voice of his elder daughter—a voice seldom heard, because he usually looked the other way. On the rare occasions they fought, he would lock himself in his room and review a lifetime of suffering—poverty, war, his parents, whom I hated horribly. Cleo always went to him, knowing his sorrow wasn't to be taken lightly. She'd knock on his door and it wouldn't be long before I would hear them engaged in one of their long, philosophical talks, which my father desperately needed. Still, Cleo always got her way. The eyes stayed.

With my mother, the clattering of pots and pans said it all. She and Cleo had a history of bickering—over glitter nail polish, skimpy outfits, barefoot boyfriends—but these days she wasn't saying much. Her own history of fleeing her North Korean homeland as a child had left her feeling helpless as an adult. Deciding which bunch of scallions to pick at the A&P could put her in a panic. Once they were picked, she still fretted, sometimes turning the cart back around.

My parents had come to America in 1954 so that my father could go to graduate school and study public administration. It was to be a temporary stay, but my father's ambitions were thwarted by the overthrow of Korean president Syngman Rhee. The political climate was too dangerous for a former aide who had his eye on the presidency himself one day. So he began a life here as a transportation economist at the World Bank in the nation's capital and started a family in the Virginia suburbs. It wasn't the life of his dreams, but it was noble work and he adjusted very well with his impeccable English. Most Americans assumed he came here by way of Oxford. My mother didn't ask any questions, and although she had many housewife acquaintances, she never mastered the language. Chipmunk was munkchip, fold the clothes was hold the clothes, and when the girl next door asked to borrow a pitcher, she came back to the door with a baseball bat. She was lovable, through no effort of her own. All the neighbors loved Mama Moon.

A WEEK into summer break, Cleo got a job as a cashier at the Rec Room. The sign for help had read CHICK NEEDED — TALK WITH TED THE HEAD. The Rec Room sold albums, eight-track tapes, guitar picks, incense, and what they advertised as "big bad bongs." Meanwhile, I spent my days going to summer school and tutoring dyslexic twin brothers, Tim and Tom.

At night Cleo and I hung out at the pool.

"Not a word to them about me not going back to school," she warned me, turning down her transistor radio. She wore a wild Hawaiian print bikini that could fit into a thimble. "Promise me, not a peep. I'll have to break it to them gently. What's a degree from a state college like Dumbo U going to do for me anyway?" She looked at me like I'd have an answer. I did, from the pages of *American Teen*.

"You need a college degree," I said, even though I'd die a million deaths if she left. "You need it to get a good job, Cleo," I said.

"Cleopatra." She batted her painted eyes.

"Cleopatra," I said.

"I'm not cut out for college. I'm not a genius like you. Einstein with pierced ears."

"No, I'm not."

"Yes, you are! You'll go to some Ivy League school and become something greater than the whole bourgeois universe put together."

"No," I stammered.

"Right now, right this second, under this ho-hum hick sky, you may be li'l Marcy Moon, but someday I'll look up and say, 'There's my superstar sister, beaming over us mere mortals.'"

"No, I'm nobody, I'm—"

She frowned. "Who?"

I almost did the unthinkable: reveal my nickname at school. Miss Moonface. Down the hallway, on the bus, in the cafeteria. *Miss Moonface, Miss Moonface, Miss Moonface.*

"I'm nobody special," I said.

"Bull! You've got God-given smarts! Why do you think you're already taking Algebra II and teaching Mit and Mot that Z ain't A? Not everybody can write a paper in French on *Waiting for Godot* watching *Welcome Back, Kotter* and reading teenybopper magazines."

"But I study a lot, Cleo."

"*Cleopatra,*" she sang impatiently.

"Cleopatra," I said.

"Well, I study, too, and I flunked chem lab. Blew away my dreams of being a mad scientist!"

·   ·   ·

CLEO MADE fun of my *American Teen* magazines—two years of back issues on my bed—but I learned about love from "Dear Romeo & Juliet," fashion from "Suit Yourself," and life from "Socrates Speaks." Ever since my only friend and song-writing partner, Meg Campbell, moved to Texas the March before, *American Teen* had been my sole source of companionship. Until Cleo came back, of course, and by then I was hooked.

MEG AND I were determined to write what we coined the Song of the Century. Someday. But now that she was gone and the M&Ms were broken up, all I had was our B songs to remember her by.

SOMEDAY, ONE DAY

Someday, one day
I shall leave this place forever
and find my hopes and dreams
Someday, one day.
I want to laugh
I want to cry
I want to live
I want to die
So that I can be free
So that I can be me.

WORD OF Cleo in her bikini got out and in no time she had so many boyfriends at the pool I couldn't count them. They would go out to her Mustang and make out like mad and do who knows what—how could I tell from the snack bar? All the while she was on the lookout for Leonard, who used to dive here high as a kite.

"When's he going to show up?" she wondered, adjusting her bikini bra. "He must have heard I'm back."

A track of small red bites on her neck silenced me. I think I will always equate the smell of chlorine on a warm summer night to the first time I smelled sex.

She flopped around in her pool chair like a lovesick fish. "I miss him, Marcy. No one comes close to loving me as much as Leonard."

"He'd cut off his ponytail, burn his guitar, and shoot old ladies if you told him to," I said.

"He'd die for me, li'l one. Up and die. But I guess I really hurt him, didn't I? The thought of me with Chuck Boucher did a number on him, didn't it?"

"It broke him in two," I assured her.

PORCELAIN DOLLS and delicate flowers—symbols of Oriental grace and beauty. But Cleo was no fragile object. She was statuesque, built to command the sun and the moon and the atmosphere on earth. Her hair was mink, and she wore it like a coat. People were stunned when they saw her, as though she had just walked out of a painting and into Drug Fair. Males were often moved to utter something, anything, even some Neanderthal grunt, as if otherwise they'd lose their chance forever. I remember an older guy with beer breath approaching us at the salad bar at Ponderosa Steak House and saying to her, "Miss, I'm a happily married man with four kids, but I just wanted you to know you're a breathtaking woman."

I never dreamed of that power myself. It was not within my realm of dreaming. If God gave me smarts, He gave her looks for two. Cleo was always saying my turn was next. But I knew it would never happen, not in this lifetime. There was only one Cleo.

A S P E C I A L summer edition of *American Teen* hit the newsstands. It was a double issue, jam-packed with gossip, fashion, and celebrity interviews. The first annual "Dream On" essay contest was also announced. The topic? *Whatever you dream on.* The grand-prize winner would have her essay and photograph published in the next year's Valentine's Day issue. I pictured my face in there, surrounded by a lacy heart. I read the announcement over and over. *Calling all American Teens! Send your most heartfelt essay with a recent photo.*

Write the winning essay—could I do it? I wanted to be part of *American Teen.* Even the notion of it hurt worse than any growing pain. But did I have a dream? What did I dream on?

F R O M A poster taped up in the window of the Rec Room, Cleo discovered that Leonard was now playing guitar in a band called EZ Times in a Georgetown bar. She got into the habit of dropping me off at home and cruising down there with some guy she'd just met at the pool. Her plan? To drive Leonard mad with jealousy. I would wait up for her, dreaming on.

"Marcy?"

Cleo cracked open my bedroom door. It was especially late; I woke up in a bed of magazines; she was talking. Beer on her breath gave her away. In the moonlight from my window all I could see were those eyes. Cleopatra eyes.

"He still ignores me. He sees me on the dance floor with other guys and he just ignores me, like I'm smoke in the air."

"Maybe he didn't see you dancing," I said.

"*Everybody* sees me."

"Maybe he's afraid of getting hurt again. Maybe he's afraid to love you again."

"He once told me if I ever left him he'd come crawling back to me on his hands and knees on a bed of nails," she said bitterly.

"Hey, Cleo, want to take a quiz in *American Teen*? It's called 'How to Tell When He Really Loves You.' Let me get it," I said, going for the light.

"No!" Cleo gasped. "Don't turn it on!"

But it was too late. It was on, and before she switched it back off I got a blinding glimpse of Cleo in another light. Her hair was a knotted mess and her lips were swollen from too much French kissing and drinking and a host of other activities I'd never learn from "Dear Romeo & Juliet."

Now she was whispering, "Shhh. . ."

My father was going downstairs. His steps were as slow and heavy as those of a man in chains. We froze, listening for clues in the dark—how many times had we done this? His bouts of insomnia kept us awake, too. But that night he let out a monstrous groan, then broke down as if there were no one else in the house. Cleo sobered up, just like that. She ran to the bathroom, combed her hair, and splashed her face with water until she had washed away her drowsiness, her drunkenness, her love for Leonard. She rushed down the steps while I sat at the top of the staircase. In a minute, my mother joined me. She was a ghost, clutching my hand. Moving as one, we inched down a few steps until we were close enough to spy on them.

"Dad, what's wrong?"

His voice could crack a wall. "Nothing. Go to bed now."

Cleo eyed a blue airmail letter in his hands. We had grown up believing *Par Avion* spelled bad news. "What do they want now? Besides your bank account?"

"Don't judge them, Cleo. For most of their lives they were poor. In spirit, they're still needy."

"*Greedy*, Dad, not needy. *Greedy!*"

"I said, don't judge them! Do you know how it feels to go to bed hungry every night? Do you know how it feels to wonder whether you will eat or starve the next day?"

"Nope," she said without apology.

"Try to understand them, Cleo. To my parents, more money means more security."

"Dad, don't kid yourself. This isn't about money." Cleo's voice matured out of nowhere. "It's just that they were born without the heart and soul you're famous for. They'll never appreciate all you do for them. They've never congratulated you when you've gotten a promotion, have they? They've never even sent you a birthday card! All they want is more, more, more. More money, more gifts, more sacrificial rites from you."

"You expect me to let them starve?"

"No! Of course not! Give them all you want! Give them your bank account! Just don't give them your heart and soul. They'll never give it back. *We're* your family—Mom and me and Marcy. We're the ones who count."

Cleo hugged my father so hard he caved in to waves of torment. They came from so deep within him they nearly knocked me over, especially at this hour. My mother squeezed my hand; her pain traveled from her heart into mine like a splinter. Still, our pain was so small compared with my father's. He cried in Cleo's arms for a long time.

I WORSHIPED Cleo more than God in those days, for her aura in the outside world, and for her bond within the walls of our house. It was only natural that she became the focus of my "Dream On" essay. Not that I ever dreamed of being Cleo—I was just her li'l hobo sister—but I did dream of being by her side in her red Mustang, suspended in time. Cleo and me, shifting into gear.

BY NOW Cleo was following Leonard from bar to bar. She was strung out on the memory of his love. I don't know how I got the nerve, but one day I looked up Leonard Lewandowski in the telephone book and called him.

"She's fucked up," he said dryly. "Tell her to stay the hell away from me."

"No she's not! She's not fucked up!" My own swearing shocked me. "She's not," I added.

"Then why's she following me around?"

"You had a romance with her."

"A romance? Give me a break! We went out a few times! Partied!"

"But you said you loved her."

"If I did, I didn't mean it. Look, I'm sorry, kid. But your sister's got problems. Get her off my ass." He hung up.

I T R I E D. I read Cleo advice from "Dear Romeo & Juliet." She yawned. I begged her to at least wave to Owen down the street, who spent every weekend washing his car, hoping for just one private moment under the stars with her. Once he even washed and waxed her Mustang until it outshone the sun. She rolled her eyes. Still, I would never tell her I called Leonard. Part of what was Cleo was what she wanted us to see.

I T W A S on a hot, muggy night—the air conditioner was broken, windows were open, portable fans were blowing—that I saw more than what I wanted to see. Cleo was out, as usual. My parents were across the street at the Sullivans'. An anniversary party, I believe. I was on my bed working on my essay and listening to some of Cleo's albums on loan from the Rec Room—Weather Report, Fleetwood Mac, and Steely Dan, my favorite. Just rocking and sweating the night away.

I thought it was a burglar, but it was just Cleo, home early. She stood in my doorway dressed in jeans, black stiletto sandals, and a sapphire-blue sequined halter. A blind man could tell she was good-looking and stone drunk. She staggered in, stood over me with the wrath of God, and uttered, "You stupid little shit."

My mind went blank.

"How could you do such a stupid little shit thing?"

"Do what, Cleo?"

"Don't play dumb with me! I know you called Leonard! Why? Why'd you do it?"

"I just wanted him to love you again," I blurted. "Please don't be mad at me, Cleo."

"*Cleopatra!*" she moaned murderously.

"Cleopatra. Sorry."

"Where did you ever get the stupid little shit idea to do such a stupid little shit thing?" She squinted contemptuously at me, then at my mountain of magazines. "From those?"

"No," I said.

"Good, because I've got news for you. You can dream for a lifetime—dream on, dream on, dream on, li'l one!—because you're not going to win any damn 'Dream On' contest! They'll take one look at your picture and toss your essay in the trash!"

"That's not true!"

Cleo began flipping through magazine after magazine. "Do you see your face in here? Because I don't!" Now she was ripping out pages, one after the other. The fan blew them in a fury across my room. "All I see in here are blue-eyed blonds!"

"That's not true!" I cried again.

"Face it, Marcy! You're not an American teen! And you never will be! Just look in the mirror!"

She dragged me to the mirror like some ugly rag doll. Whatever she was saying hadn't hit me yet. All I saw was the stark difference between us. Cleo, gorgeously wasted in sequins. Me, so pitifully plain in an old smock top.

How could we be sisters?

She stumbled in place. "Don't dream on about being with me. Look at me, I'm a fucking mess!"

Dizziness got the best of her and she sank to my bed. Her painted eyelids were magnificently winged tonight and they fluttered up and down with confession.

"Leonard never loved me, okay? He never even liked me. And you know why? Because I look more like some mama-san in the rice paddies than good old Aunt Bea, that's why. I'm not good enough for Leonard. Oh, I'm good enough to screw till he's blue in the face, but not good enough to meet his fucking white-bread family. I swear to God, if I ever see his gross-out face again, I'll strangle him with his own ponytail! Do you understand what I'm talking about? Do you?"

This was not Cleo talking. Not the Cleo I knew. My Cleo never knew the chill of inferiority, up and down the spine. The cruel valentines and lonely lunches. The Miss Moonface down the hallway, on the bus. *Miss Moonface, Miss Moonface, Miss Moonface.* Not Cleo, who carried herself like the queen of jeans.

"Do you have any idea what I'm talking about?" she whined before passing out.

"No," I lied.

IN THE morning—the aftermath—Cleo lay in my bed like volcanic ashes. It was over. She was asleep when I inched in, having already been to summer school and back. When she opened her eyes, it almost got me crying. Somehow her eyeliner had smeared off during the sweaty night and I remembered who she was. My big sister at the wheel.

"What am I doing here?" she groggily asked.

"You got drunk last night. You passed out on my bed. I called the Rec Room to tell them you were sick. They said, 'Far out.'"

"Wow"—she rubbed her forehead—"the whole night's a blur." She tried to get up but her hangover won out and she sank back into my pillow with a smile.

"So, what do you feel like doing today, li'l one?"

BY AFTERNOON, her hangover was gone and those Cleopatra eyes were back on. All that was left was a headache, easily remedied by a cruise in her Mustang. The top was down and the streaked sky matched her tie-dyed tank top. She shifted into gear.

"Hang on!"

We zipped onto the Beltway, radio on, guys going wacko.

Slow down, foxy lady!

You're a thousand on a scale of one to ten!

You ain't built like a brick wall!

Why couldn't it always be this way? Eternal adoration on a never-ending highway. Cleo and me, playing hooky from life.

"Are we going to Taco Town?" I wondered.

"Taco Town?" she scoffed. "I don't want any memories of that messed-up dude!"

Cleo pulled off an exit and into a shopping center. Her Mustang came to a screeching halt in front of the Fotobooth. The Fotobooth?

"What are we doing here?" I asked her.

Her sunglasses slid down her nose and razzle-dazzled me into her spell.

"Have you lost your mind, li'l one? It's time to get your picture taken for the contest!"

AFTER A few shots of me alone, Cleo joined me in the booth. We must have spent an hour in there, monkeying around. That hour captured a funny strip of life: There's me at fourteen, sticking my tongue out. And there's Cleo at nineteen, pouting her Wet 'n' Wild lips. Now she's got her chin on my head like some skull-crushing monster. We're both cross-eyed and crammed so close together it's hard to tell who's who.

3

CLEO STRETCHES like a Persian cat before a French window in the breakfast room.

"Weekends in the summer are what living on the Bay is all about. Let the sunshine in!"

That strikes me as a strange thing to say the day after Stu's funeral. But who can really hear what's going on in Cleo's mind? Besides, the phone is ringing. Again.

"I'm not taking one more sympathy call, no way!" Cleo cries. "Every Tom, Dick, and Harry who knew Stu since P.S.-who-cares has called! I don't want every Tom, Dick, and Harry bothering me!"

But I wonder whether this is true. Getting too much attention was always Cleo's forte.

"I've got to run now," Cleo says, gathering things. "The mess I left in the office is waiting for me." She's sporting a yellow tennis outfit with white deck shoes. Not a thread of black. "Can you feed the baby, Marcy? Her bottle's already warmed up in the microwave."

"Sure," I say. "Where is she?"

"Napping in the nook on the staircase landing."

"Isn't that an odd place to put her?"

"Are you kidding? June Moon likes it there. The sun streams through the skylight and puts a smile on her face while she sleeps," Cleo explains. "On cloudy days she makes me move her back to her bedroom."

Who's *Cleo* kidding? She sets June Moon down like a rubber plant and claims to read her mind.

"I should be home in the late afternoon. We'll do the family thing, drag Luke away from his computer and analyze him byte by byte. Afterward, you can tell me what your magic brain waves are telling you," she says.

"Where is Luke, anyway? I haven't seen him all morning."

"Where else? At Pier Pressure, playing his favorite game."

"Suicide Spell." I cringe.

"He'll wander in at some point and expect lunch, even if it's four o'clock. That's how he is these days—why do you think the nanny left without notice? Then he'll go into his bedroom and hole up in cyberspace. It's depressing."

How can Cleo go to sleep, much less go to the office? If he were mine, I'd take him out on a starry night and make him speak to himself.

"I'll try talking to him," I say. "But Cleo, please don't expect magic here, okay?"

"I have to," she says, sulking. "There's nothing worse than feeling your own child pull away from you. Whatever you say or do is dust. Now I know what I put Mom through. At least the language barrier was on my side; she couldn't bitch in English. Although I suspect she cussed me out in Korean a time or two."

Whenever I call up my mother's image I see a woman about to fall to her knees in a bleak light through our kitchen window. That woman may remain there in my memories, but now she lives at the Hanguk Home for the Aged in Los Angeles. For thirty years I watched her play silent, anguished games of Solitaire. Group games like Changi and Yut only drove her deeper into her game. Now she's the Changi champ of the Hanguk Home, all smiles. Well, she was always happier with her own kind. Which Cleo and I were not quite. Whenever I call her, she tells me she almost forgets she's in America. At the Hanguk Home, no one speaks English, no one eats American food except for Jell-O cubes which they gobble down with chopsticks. It's like she—the person she was meant to be—picked up where she left off, a few years before the Korean War.

"Only my hair now pure white," she cheerfully repeats over and over.

She did not make it to Stu's funeral. Too far, was her excuse. But even if she lived at the Hanguk Home for the Aged in San Francisco, she probably wouldn't have come.

"How is she, anyway?" Cleo asks. She's hurt, but unentitled.

"She spends all day watching Korean soap operas. At night she plays Changi, Yut, and Omok."

"Omok," Cleo echoes. "I've probably forgotten how to play."

· · ·

CLEO INCHED back into my life after the Hanguk Home sent her an invitation to our mother's sixty-fifth birthday party. Talk about a surprise! Cleo is walking through the door after eighteen years. Not a flicker of emotion did I feel that day. And if I did, I put it out so fast sparks died on the spot.

FOR THE first time since my arrival Friday night, I look at Cleo not in a light long gone but in the San Francisco morning light, which falls objectively on her face while she ponders our mother's absence. I am, was always fated to be, the plain one, the homely one, which I now embrace, for there is something to be said for a simple existence. Wake up, braid my hair, carry on. But Cleo still has what drives men mad and women madder. And all the years of drugs and drink and sex have left their own villainous beauty mark on her. No, she wouldn't cause the commotion she once did in Mount Sorak when the Korean police ordered her to put her hair up in a ponytail and wear long pants. This was a resort, women were swimming nude in the lake, but they couldn't make a ripple what with Cleo walking by in a pair of denim cutoffs, hair swinging off her hips. The whole mountain shook with her indecent exposure. Oh, she was so secretly pleased with herself.

I'm not saying Cleo hasn't aged. She's no longer a nineteen-year-old girl making waves. But she's still got what women want and what men want more.

She has, however, given up smoking and a tongue that could sharpen nails. No way could she spit red-hot obscenities to a car cutting her off anymore. The Petunia-bashing is a thing of the past; that fire has been put out.

Today, it seems, Cleo has other fires to tend. Cleo's Creations. The Global Gourmet Food Show. But where does that leave her children? Who tends to them?

THE BAY has come to life with bobbing activity. But what do I do with myself in this playland? In White Sky, I have place, purpose, Cactus Bear. I know that for every pair of moccasins I ring up, I'm feeding a beautiful baby with smoky black eyes. Sell a sand painting, and a family eats supper for a week. Even when business is slow and Pablo and I are playing Omok, I'm busy walking my Moccathon, straight into a sun that sets in my eyes. Walking, walking, walking.

JUNE MOON takes me on a tour of her house. What a bundle she is, so warm and powdery. Pablo would be so jealous. His dream is to hold a White Sky baby, knowing it is ours forever. He wants to wrap it up in a blanket woven of moons and stars. He romanticizes this baby, he wants someone to hold harder than me.

I follow her drooling chin from room to room. A dizzy experience of antiques, teakwood, statues, gaudy paintings. Sitting rooms, sun rooms, alcoves. Rooms with the same views from slightly different angles. What mind decorated all these rooms? Cleo's, of course.

If I asked her to donate this junk and feed a few homeless mouths, she'd probably call them bums and whistle on her way. Well, I bet she's forgotten who would have crawled around the village of Yong Pyong naked if not for the Salvation Army. And I bet she's forgotten who graduated from college in sneakers from Goodwill.

Yes, from the looks of things around here—or not here—I bet Cleo has forgotten our father.

He has, conveniently, slipped her mind. Unlike the oversized mother-of-pearl vase wedged between a leather love seat and iron bookshelf, she seems to have no place for him. Pablo would stop this train of thought in its tracks right now. He believes that it's better to have only one good eye; then you don't look too deeply.

"Why cause brain strain?" he says.

But I must see Cleo for who she really is. Bathed in natural light, her darkness might take form. I can't fall for Cleo as I once did; don't want to curve out of reality and think the sun is the moon and a blackout is a celestial sky. Once she may have cared about our father, but it wasn't everlasting love. Her emotions stay this side of the grave. The proof lies in this house of priceless junk. Not a hint of our father exists here. No sentimental dust falls on a single photograph.

J U N E   M O O N has a squat Buddha body and hair so black it flashes white. Her eyes are mysterious paper cutouts. On closer inspection, though, her hair has wave and her nose has point, and by the time she goes to school, her Oriental look will have waned. That has already happened to Luke, whose brown hair casts blond in the summer. His face is tan and Asiatic, but his bones are European, long and lean.

IN THE middle of a marvelous meditation—I'm cross-legged on the kitchen floor, facing the sun, chanting "Cactus Bear" to myself—a shadow crosses over me. I sense the shadow with reluctance, for I don't fall in so deeply every day. Escapism does it; meditation is the perfect vehicle home. I open my eyes. It's Luke. With his slumped posture, he displays his indifference to me.

"Where's June Moon?"

"Napping."

"Where?"

"In her room."

We're total strangers, Luke and I. I've always been aloof to the idea of him and have never given him a second thought. He was Cleo's, nothing to me. But now I see Luke at thirteen in the flesh and he is real to me, a kid who can't make eye contact.

"Luke, why don't you join me in a moment of meditation?"

He frowns. "What for?"

"To find the center of your soul and make peace with it."

"No, thanks."

"Okay," I say, going under.

He is watching me; his angst crawls all over me like bugs. This time I keep my eyes closed.

"What are you doing?" he says.

"I told you, Luke, finding the center of my soul."

"Why?"

"I'm going on a Moccathon and I can't go the distance until my soul is ready for the challenge."

"What's a Moccathon?"

"A charity walkathon."

"Get on a treadmill," he says. "We've got two in the exercise room."

"It's a spiritual walk, not a physical walk. If my heart and soul are ready, I'll be able to walk forever."

"You need medication, not meditation," he mutters under his breath.

I hear him walking away; my desire to draw him in has failed.

"Luke!" I cry out.

"What?"

"How are you doing?"

"Okay."

"When my dad died, I went under for so long I forgot to come back up. Sometimes I think I'm still trying to come back up. Do you know what I'm saying?"

"Stu wasn't my real dad."

His stone-cold stare shivers me out of any meditative state. Cactus Bear must wait.

"Is there something on your mind, Luke? Because if there is, I'm all ears."

"Yeah. Why are you still here?"

.   .   .

LUKE ISN'T black-hearted like Cleo. He's just stoned on sadness. What's he so sad about? A mystery father, haunting his thoughts? A stepfather, now dead? A mother who neglects his needs?

OVER A lunch of brown rice and beans I say, "I'm going to be honest with you, Luke."

He stews into his food, ready to erupt.

"Your mom wanted me to stay here after the funeral because she's worried about you."

Luke points at his food with his fork. "What's this?"

"Humble food brings people down to their knees," I inform him.

"Why? So they can pray for prime rib?"

"*Meat* is a four-letter word. Besides, bread and water is better."

"This is rice and beans," he flatly states.

"I'm speaking figuratively."

"I figure I'm not hungry."

"Basic food feeds basic thought, which nourishes basic talk."

"Who can talk when they're busy barfing? Besides, there's nothing to talk about."

"What are you talking about, there's nothing to talk about? There are worlds to talk about! Oceans and mountains and skies. I mean the ones in your gut, Luke!"

He gets up with a bored sigh, opens the cupboard. "My gut wants Cleo's Creations."

"No, Luke!" I shout.

"Why not?"

"Don't poison what's natural. Don't lose what's real!"

"My mom makes a *real* fortune with her sauces," he says, mocking me.

LATER, OUT of the corner of his mouth, he says, dryly, "So what happens when you find the center of your soul?"

"I say 'Cactus Bear.'"

"What does that mean?"

"Well, it's the name of my shop in White Sky, Nevada. And it means 'All's Well.'"

Luke doesn't hide his disgust. The boy is not a believer.

"Well," he blurts out, "all's *not* well here."

"Okay. Let's talk about it, Luke. What's not well here?"

"You mean besides the food?"

I detect in Luke someone who has cracked open the door, even though I've always been a distant aunt—and who knows what else, according to his mother. The fact that he's sitting down and eating with me, brooding but still eating, is worth a small hand clap. True, he poured on the sauce—something so peppery red I swear I saw smoke—but at least we met in the struggle.

"Are you like anti-sauce or something?" he asks.

"Why mask the natural state of food?"

"To make it eatable."

"It's eatable all by itself," I argue.

"Are you like anti-salt and -pepper, too?"

"They're okay, they're cheap, but I don't have much use for them."

"My mom says you're so poor you wear old hand-me-downs."

"Not poor compared with a lot of people, Luke. You want to see poor, come home with me."

He shrugs.

THAT LUKE won't look me in the eye or call me by name is not his fault. His sad orphan aura won't quit. There are, I understand, scores of stepcousins on Stu's side, but as Cleo tells it, Stu's parents didn't approve of his marrying a non-Jew and a Korean at that. They were so appalled they kept the relatives at bay, and Luke grew up an only child, until June Moon came along.

But Luke's real tragedy is that he's holding something back. In his thirteen-year-old mind, it is earth-shattering. Bigger than the both of us.

If Luke were in White Sky, he could take in the silent stars and clear his head with one sigh. Maybe he would feel at home and stay.

4

THE NEIGHBORHOOD we lived in was typical of the times: split-level houses, tricycles turned over, no crime to speak of. In the winter we shoveled our driveway; in the summer we watered our lawn. Our house was cedar-shingled with tan shutters. It sat majestically on a small hill, unlike the other homes, which sat squatly on flat lawns. Our lot had thick woods, too, and our back yard blended into a wilderness of birds bathing and leaves swirling. I could not imagine growing up in any other place, among any other people. It was the only world I knew.

And yet I knew little of the world my parents had come from. I'd hear them whispering in their mysterious tongue and run for cover. Run for my life! Their world was smoke from a bomb, shrapnel, someone else's history, not mine. It was not spelled out for me and, like the language, not taught to me. It was a black cloud over the other side of the globe my father had given

me for my tenth birthday. Their world was so far away I could
spin it out of my mind with "Movie Star Makeovers" in *American Teen* magazine. *Skimpy lashes? Powder them first, then apply
Maybelline mascara with long, sweeping strokes.*

I had visited their world four times. Every third summer my
parents would drag Cleo and me back to our homeland, courtesy of the World Bank. Homeland? They had to drag us there
by our hair! Our grandparents' house in the outskirts of Seoul
was the Mount Vernon of their village. Meaning it was a stone
house with a toilet, a yard, and a high gate that kept the lepers
out. There was nothing to do, no water to drink, nowhere to go
without all the raggedy people pointing at us.

"We're Made in the U.S.A.," Cleo would explain.

We stayed in and played a lot of cards and Omok. Monsoon
rains were always falling.

My grandparents were too foreign to bother with. I didn't
like the way they looked, dressed, spoke, or smelled. Like pick-
led garlic and mold. Worse, they fought late at night, every
night. They were cruel to their young maid, who slept in a
closet off the kitchen. My grandmother beat her silly for stealing Cleo's lacy underwear, then turned around and slipped a
charm bracelet right off my wrist. With her grotesque, gold-
toothed smile she marveled over the colorful glass gems glued
onto silver clovers.

"Fake," my father told her.

"Ah." She frowned, giving it back.

Korea—*whose* homeland?—was a land of flies swarming
around dusty beggars. Bus fumes. Rotting garbage. My earliest
visits remain the most haunting, though they didn't seem so at

the time. Neither the orphan boys circling our cab at Kimpo Airport—their faces flattened up against the windows crying *gum! gum!*—nor the cloaked lepers in the mountains made me question or wonder why everyone over here had such rotten luck. From taxis I'd look out for Jeeps rumbling by for a glimpse of American soldiers and grow homesick for peanut-butter-and-jelly sandwiches.

Our only consolation was knowing that on the return trip, the family would vacation on a Hawaiian island—Oahu, Maui, the Big Island. One island was as good as another. We were back in the U.S.A.!

TIM AND Tom Duncan were my age but a grade behind me. In the second grade we had worked together on a papier-mâché project, a standing bear that looked more like a cactus than a bear. That's what Miss Delaney said, awarding our Cactus Bear with an A-plus. So beloved was our Cactus Bear that it went on exhibit in the school's display case before somebody broke in and stole it. That year in Miss Delaney's class, our A-plus was divided equally. We were equals. But somewhere along the line, Tim and Tom fell behind.

They were frail boys with pasty complexions and feathery auburn hair. They were truly identical, and what they shared more than freckles was dyslexic genes. Reading was a slow, grueling experience.

They lived in my neighborhood, a few blocks away in a small, stately colonial with manor airs. Trimmed hedges fenced them off from the rest of us. Their father, Major Duncan, was a mean man who probably went to bed in his uniform and, if he ever actually slept, dreamed of being saluted by all us peons. He kicked the whole household around, including their black toy poodle, Afro.

"Out of my way, Afro, before I stuff you!"

Poor thing, I can still see him flying up the white-carpeted stairs. The air conditioning is on too high, the house is so sterile.

A green Cadillac sat in the driveway but I never saw it move. Mrs. Duncan stayed home and drank a lot of coffee. Her face was always perfectly made up, but her expression was worn down. She had no distinct personality to speak of; meek, aggressive—both words described her. I noticed this one morning when she offered me a jelly doughnut after a particularly frustrating lesson. Tim had given up and left the kitchen table.

"They still can't get it right, Marcy. Major Duncan thinks he has all the answers. He drills them at breakfast, then blows his stack. After dinner he sets out Scrabble and drives them to tears. Guess who has to pick up the pieces?"

"But it's not their fault," I said, watching her pour another cup.

"Try telling that to the Major. The bastard blames it on me, you know. 'Tina, I come from a long line of military men and they always knew which boot they were putting on.' Lord knows where I'd like to put *his* boot!"

Mrs. Duncan was given my name by our school principal, but the truth was, I wasn't qualified to tutor Tim and Tom. Dyslexia? I could barely spell the word. What little I knew came from an article I had read in *American Teen* magazine. "Conquer Your Learning Disabilities with a Smart Attitude." Each weekday I gave Tim and Tom a reading lesson, period. I paced them slowly so they would study each word before saying it aloud, before getting all tongue-tied and defeated. Most times it didn't work, but on the rare occasion one of them got through a whole paragraph, I would hear a queer, hushed "Cactus Bear."

"Please don't tell any of your friends about our arrangement, Marcy," Mrs. Duncan said.

What friends? Meg was in Texas.

"Major Duncan would die of humiliation. And the boys, well, I don't want to make it any more difficult for them than it already is. Their classmates think they were held back because of too many sick days."

I liked my role in the Duncan household. I was their savior, their teacher. Their master, if I read between the lines. For every two-hour lesson I got six dollars and a feeling of Cleo—I was looked at in awe.

MAYBE IN my cracked little core I knew Cleo was right about *American Teen* magazine, but I finished my essay, typed it up, and mailed it along with a picture of me with my eyes half closed. No one ever claimed I was a vision of beauty, what with black straw for hair and *a face so flat Santa musta sat on it*—I'm quoting the creeps on the bus. But the editors would look beyond that, wouldn't they? A face is a face is a face, and beauty is in the eyes of the beholder, isn't it?

On a morning of mixed sunshine and clouds, I started my period. Cleo called in sick and took me to lunch at the Tiny Tea

Cup. We celebrated with wonton soup, egg rolls, and sizzling pepper steak. The sizzling plate scared me; then excited me. I broke out in a sweat; my bra was soaking wet. Was I a woman now?

After my meal I cracked open my fortune and read: *Your heart will always make itself known through words.* I believed this to be true.

I would win the contest!

Cleo wasn't as upbeat; her good mood had waned halfway through her soup. She got into vans with total strangers but the thought of telling our parents she wasn't going back to school rolled in her head like distant thunder. She crumpled her fortune into a small ball and flicked it into a crowded ashtray. She lit up a cigarette and started dropping ashes into her teacup.

"What did it say?" I asked her.

"You'll choke on a chicken bone before you're legal," she said, deadpan.

"Cleo—"

"*Cleopatra* or I'll stuff your fortune down your pretty little throat."

"Cleopatra, don't joke about your fortune. You'll jinx it. That's what Meg says her aunt says."

"Fortunes are for Sad Sacks, Marcy. For dreaming old maids who wish they could start over. For Petunias who pray some Porky will sweep them off their fat feet. For Mits and Mots who don't know which way is up. For Ma and Pa Kettles who hope the rain will come, dang it all. But not for Cleopatra Moon," she said, gorgeously puffing. "I don't stake my fate on a scrap of paper, wishful thinking, or silly eight balls. No offense to Meg, I know she lives by that crap. The power is in me and me alone. When a good-looking guy goes by, I don't need to cross my fingers. And when he says he loves me the next day, I don't need to knock on wood."

I inched closer to Cleo, my idol, wanting her smoke and musk oil—her miraculous power—to rub off on me. Who would dare to call me Miss Moonface then?

"How many guys have told you that?" I wondered aloud. "How many guys have said 'I love you, Cleopatra Moon'?"

"More than could fill this room, li'l one," she quipped as a waiter with a tray of fragrant food walked by our booth, ogling her. She sniffed at him—what gall! He was, after all, just a little Chinese waiter. "Every guy in Theta Chi sports the same bumper sticker: *I brake for Cleo*. But the point is, eat the cookie and throw the fortune away. Whether it's a scholarship to Mount Holyoke or the Nobel Prize, nothing happens unless you make it happen. Nothing happens daydreaming on your duff."

Oh, but I liked daydreaming on my duff. Like right now, right here, in the Tiny Tea Cup as a light shower began to fall. I could see it, hear it, even smell it. It was warm and perfumed from a thousand summers past. I was singing in it, dancing in it, naked as Eve. My body was changing; I was coming alive!

MY MOTHER'S nickname sickened me with shame. A natural reaction—I had gone through the sixth grade known as Ho Chi Moon. But our neighbors didn't call her Mama Moon to be cruel; no, they loved the lady with the foreign laugh. She laughed at the drop of a hat, a car going by, a bird in the sky. What they would never dream is that, translated, her laughter would come through as a cry.

Who was she crying for? For three older brothers killed in three different wars. Her youngest brother was recruited by the Japanese to fight the Americans in World War II. He never returned home and was presumed dead. Her middle brother was living outside Shanghai when his whole village—including his family, a wife and three little ones—was slaughtered during the Chinese Civil War. Her oldest and favorite brother met his fate on the same night he had taken her out to a fancy Western restaurant. Over pork cutlets and coleslaw, he had explained that although the Korean War had not officially broken out, it was imminent. He would be traveling south later that evening to Pusan, where many Koreans were taking refuge. Eventually, he said, the two of them would meet up there. But this was not to be: North Korean Communists murdered him en route to Pusan.

My mother spent many an afternoon praying for these unlucky brothers, whose strange names I could never remember, though she muttered them over and over again so God wouldn't forget them. She was crying, too, for a saint of a father I never met, rumored dead but not properly buried. Most of all, she was crying for a mother—whereabouts unknown in North Korea—she'd give me up for. That's what she told me once in a crying rage—said it without thinking, Cleo explained. Mama Moon, our neighbors called her. What did they know? What did I care? So she got out of North Korea in the nick of time. She'd give me up for her mother, wouldn't she?

My mother's past was a shadow, a gray area. No microscope could pick up all the thoughts that moved around in her mind or all the thoughts that diseased it. Cleo said she was a complex woman who was unable to express herself in words, but could I really buy that?

"I'm afraid to tell Mom I started my period," I told her as we pulled away from the Tiny Tea Cup. "She warned me not to start until I was sixteen, like her. Why does she say things like that?"

"Look," Cleo said, "she spoke Korean at home and Jap at school under Jap rule—it wasn't exactly *Romper Room*, okay? They don't call Japs murdering monkeys for nothing. She had to pretend she was someone she wasn't in mind, body, and spirit. She had a Jap name, Okawa Toshiko, she saluted the Jap flag, and she prayed to a Jap god by the name of Emperor Hiro*shito*. But at home she went back to who she really was. Eunook Kim, playing Yut and Omok and singing Korean hymns.

"Just before the war broke out, she secretly crossed the thirty-eigthth parallel, *sans* folks—they were waiting for son number-three to come home from the war, gambling on time, a peaceful outcome. Sometimes faith is a curse; she never saw her folks again and son number-three never came home. Then she got married, came here, and had to learn another lingo. Toss in shock, anger, and the fact that she's got a bit of Mit and Mot in her and you've got Mom."

I was looking through rain, listening to Cleo. Somehow the rain made it so real, so vivid. My mother's history had always been a blurry sketch to me. Now it came alive in vibrant color. I could picture her doing all those things in an ancient, cinematic rain. But what did that have to do with the fact that she didn't seem to love me then, in 1976?

"You can fuck the whole world, li'l one, but you've got to forgive your parents," Cleo said, dropping me off at home. Then she was off to the cabin where people partied twenty-four hours a day.

O u r   k i t c h e n was small but airy, with yellow linoleum countertops and matching floors. A colorful Korean calendar hung next to the telephone like a window to the past, while a bay window brought in the backyard.

My mother stood over a pot of boiling meat. A mound of precisely sliced scallions sat on the cutting board. It was only midafternoon, but supper was in the works.

"Mom, guess what?"

She didn't bother to look up. "Guess what?"

"I started my period," I said.

She said nothing, stirring the pot with a long lacquer spoon. My mother had survived bombs over her head but sometimes the clear blue sky brought her down.

"Mom, I said I started my period."

"Don't be like your sister," she warned me. "Don't run around with ugly, long-haired hippie boys."

"I won't," I said.

"People look down on her like Saigon bar girl."

"No one looks down on Cleo!" I argued. "Everybody thinks she's the most beautiful girl in the world! I've heard them say so!"

She murmured, stirring doubtfully as sweat beaded on her temple.

"So what most beautiful mean? Boy supposed to pick you up at front door like a lady, not horn honk! That disgrace. You better than that, Marcy. You number-one student, no B's. Always remember, brain come first. Beauty not much count."

Sometimes, like then, I tired of all that. If I was so smart, how come I had called Leonard Lewandowski? If I was so smart, how come I couldn't get Tim and Tom to see straight? Besides, I'd give up half my brains for half of Cleo's beauty.

My mother turned down the stove, went upstairs, and returned with something for me. It was a small gift box wrapped in floral paper. Inside I found a bottle of Love's Baby Soft cologne. I cradled it, silenced by her show of affection.

"I'll wear it every day, Mom."

But my mother didn't seem to hear me. Something had upset her; she was shaking.

"Mom, what's wrong?"

"Daddy going away again on mission."

"That's not fair! He just got back!" I wailed. He had been gone all spring in South America, leaving my mother and me behind in the house. Our creaking footsteps had grown louder every night. "Where's he going this time?"

"You name it, he going. Indonesia, Thailand, India, Singapore. End up in Korea to see good-for-nothing parents. Two months gone, help whole world, not own family," she said.

The World Bank sent my father on missions to underdeveloped countries six months out of the year, at least. News that he was leaving again always set a moan in motion. We needed him more than other families needed their fathers.

Although my mother had gotten her learner's permit the same day as Cleo—by quizzing her, she memorized the manual—she had never actually learned how to drive. When my father was away she had no choice but to rely on our neighbors to take her to the A&P. Mrs. Neumann with the white Buick wagon. Mrs. McDougal with the sky-blue Pinto her college daughter had left behind. Neighbors, but not friends. Like many English words, "friends" was not in her vocabulary. My mother would thank them profusely with a smile that went dead the minute she walked back in the door. Then she would proceed to pray for hours on end. For my father's health, for good meals on the airplane, for sober pilots.

My father, in turn, worried about us every minute he was away. In airports and hotels, in meetings and dinners his thoughts always traveled back to our house. Letters and postcards were in the mailbox every day.

"Now that Cleo's back, she can drive you to the A&P, Mom," I pointed out.

"In Torino, no Mustang," she warned me. "Mustang dangerous, should throw in garbage can."

"She can take us to the Korean store, too. She knows the way," I said.

CLEO WAS fired from the Rec Room the next day. Ted the Head said she wasn't taking her job seriously, that they weren't paying her three-fifty an hour for nursing hangovers. On her way out, she dropped a bucket of guitar picks in the trash and busted a few stereo needles.

That afternoon she got a job at Songs & Bongs, which was billed as "The Music Store for the Hard Core." Groups like the Damned and the Wrecked 'n' Ragged hung out in the back room, writing songs and polishing bongs. My parents were keen on the idea of Cleo working at Songs & Bongs.

"Song and Bong are both Korean names," my father mused.

MANY HOURS of my adolescence were spent willing gory deaths on Frog Fitzgerald. Frog, thrown off the Octopus, trampled by the crowd, and swept under the tent with the lions—all during lunch period. For his insolent drawl alone, such punishment was deserved. "Hello, Miss Moonface" the moment I stepped onto the bus. "Bye-bye, Miss Moonface" the moment I stepped off. I was questioning God in those days with a big black question mark: If there truly was a God, why was He—along with Frog Fitzgerald—always picking on me?

One hot steamy day I was walking home from Tim and Tom's minding my own business when Frog pulled up beside me on a blue moped. He was bad news in a torn muscle T-shirt and frayed jeans that dragged on the street.

"Going my way?"

I walked on as though he didn't exist, keeping my spongy armpits to myself. I was walking so stone-faced the pavement almost cracked. If Cleo had been there she'd have frayed his balls with one look.

Why wasn't she there?

"Looks like you finally outgrew your training bra." He laughed obscenely, so hard his shaggy brown hair went in every direction.

Frog was used to being the center of the universe, especially when the universe was a school bus. Now, in broad daylight, on a street called Wandering Lane, he didn't like being ignored. With a deafening *vroom vroom*, he jumped the curb and blocked my path.

"Want to go in the woods for a smoke? Got a pack of Marlboros we can kill."

Fear clutched me in the throat like the Boston Strangler. Where was Cleo? Cleo! Without her, I was just the mute on the bus. It took every ounce of courage for me to utter, "Go croak, Frog."

He laughed horribly and took off in a cloud of conceit. To the whole deserted street he did a Jimmy Durante: "Miss Moonface loves me!"

LIKE A lost dog I wandered home. *Miss Moonface loves me?* What did Frog mean? Was he dyslexic, too? I didn't love him any more than squished worms in the driveway! He was uglier than any frog I'd ever seen. A Frog was a Frog was a Frog forever. Right?

By the time I got home I was drunk with confusion, bumping into walls like Cleo late at night. On some quest for truth I frantically searched through recent issues of *American Teen*. A new column, "Wonder Girl in the Universe," attempted to connect readers to truths *like stars in constellations* by answering questions like *Is there such a thing as love at first sight? If I kiss two boys, does that make me a bad person? Is puppy love for real?* None of the questions was my question.

What did Frog mean?

Miss Moonface loves me.

I looked in my mirror. A girl looked back at me, blinking. A plain girl. A girl in need of a long, deep kiss that would leave her shivering and changed forever. A girl in need of a movie-star makeover.

I backed up and stood sideways. Even through a baggy T-shirt, they bulged out. Pulsed out. When did they grow? When I was sleeping? Dreaming? Eating beef 'n' bean burritos?

I sneaked into Cleo's room—a perfumed pigsty!—and sifted through a drawer flooded with bras and bikini underwear and scarf-sized halter tops. I made my choice, a halter constructed of no more than three strings and a triangle of black silk. With great orchestration I fit it on, then stood before Cleo's heart-shaped brass mirror where she drew on her eyes every morning.

Bye-bye, Miss Moonface!

THIS GOT to be a habit, whenever Cleo left the house. She was gone most of the time these days, working at Songs & Bongs or partying with the lead singer from the Degenerates who played in a club called After Hours in Old Town, Alexandria. Who knows why Cleo never had a curfew. Maybe my parents thought she was going through a stage. Or maybe they'd rather be asleep when she stumbled in.

Anyway, I'd sneak into Cleo's room and transform myself in faded denim and glittery black. I'd slip off my faded pink moccasins and slip on her silver sandals and strut my stuff against walls covered with Led Zeppelin posters. If Frog saw me like this he'd wipe out and beg for one more long, lingering look. If he were in the path of a dump truck, I'd quit questioning God.

Eventually I graduated to Cleo's lipsticks. She kept discarded tubes in a wooden cigar box my father had bought in the Philippines. Siren Red, Midnight Mauve, Peaches 'n' Cream. Swiveling the lipstick up from its tube became something no less than sensual, especially when I knew what pleasure was coming next: the sexy smear across my lips.

Only one Cleopatra Moon could walk this earth and part the seas, but in my own right I was a woman now, too. That I tingled from head to toe told me so.

5

LIKE HER million-dollar home, Cleo is still hot property. Men have been calling for her all day without any regard for a baby trying to get some sleep. My phone phobia doesn't stop me from eavesdropping on their short, sweet messages. Their names sound conservative—Bob, Sid, Elliot—and their voices more mature than the ones I recall with names like Van, Chip, Denny. Still, I detect undertones. "Call me" means "*Call me.*" And "If there's anything you need" means "If there's *anything* you need."

I suspect that Cleo loves this. The more I listen, the more she gives herself away.

"I DON'T know what I'd do without these guys," Cleo says when she gets home.

We're in the sun room, sitting on pale-blue wicker. A light

late-afternoon shower falls outside while we drink lemonade. In another life, with another past, I might call this inspiring.

"Elliot is my prime investor, and he's helping me out of the pure goodness of his heart. He doesn't need the profits or the losses or the headaches of a young company like mine. All he really needs is a vacation, poor guy. The man is working himself to death and his wretched hag of a wife loves him for it."

I'm listening.

"He was a client of Stu's. Stu made him a hell of a lot of money. Stu made *everyone* a hell of a lot of money." Cleo tunes in to the rain, grows dreamy. "Bob is a good friend of ours, too. He's an accountant."

I'm still listening.

"He's such an angel, he's offered his services to me free of charge for the next year. After all, I'm a sauce maker, period. I balance flavors, not books."

Enough's enough. "Cleo, I honestly don't get it. Why are you risking what Stu has left you and the kids?"

"Because I'm more than what Stu left me. Yes, he made it happen, but this was my dream long before Stu came along. I started small but now I have a company that grosses more than you can possibly imagine."

"So what more do you want? Why do you need the East Coast when you've got the West Coast eating out of the palm of your hand?"

"Because that's pocket change compared to its potential," she brashly quips.

"I wouldn't call nine dollars a bottle pocket change," I remark. "Excuse me, but I call it a little insane."

Cleo keeps her cool, otherwise I'm on a bus back to White Sky and the Global Gourmet Food Show is off.

"Excuse *me*, but I'm not talking about a product for people who dine in soup kitchens, Marcy. I'm talking about a product for people who will fork out for a bottle of sauce that will make a meal go from adequate to exquisite. True, I've already opened accounts with most of the gourmet markets on the West Coast. Next stop: the whole country. And I'm going to make it happen at the Global Gourmet Food Show," she declares. "I'm blowing up all our publicity shots wall-size. I'm going to wow and woo every vendor with promises I couldn't keep in a million years. Advertising and sampling allowances. A gift-with-purchase program. Anything to get my line in the door."

My silence speaks for itself.

"You know, Marcy, it's not all about money. I'm not a money-monger. It's about me doing something with my life besides being a wife."

"I'm sorry if this sounds harsh, but don't you mean *widow*, Cleo? And besides, you're also a mother. June Moon needs your arms, Luke is cramped up with loneliness, and all you can talk about is some food show. I know we made a deal but I still can't believe you're leaving them at a time like this."

"Look," she says, "I'm leaving them for a few measly days to live out a dream. *My* dream. Do you know what that feels like?"

"Better than you know."

"So what is it? What's your dream?"

"To walk to the ends of the earth."

"Good grief," she moans. "Not that dumb walkathon."

"Moccathon."

"Whatever."

"I'm going to walk until I've covered every square inch of this earth. With your pledge, the White Sky will live forever."

DESPITE CLEO'S efforts, a family dinner is a catastrophe. June Moon is hot and bothered in her highchair, Luke wants out. It's a formal affair in the dining room. Salmon cakes with sweet-corn cilantro sauce, thanks to Bayside Gourmet. Lime-inspired water sparkling in crystal goblets. Why we're not eating cool tomato sandwiches and drinking out of paper cups on the balcony is just one reason why Cleo flunked child psych.

To her disappointment, I heated up my leftover lunch.

"I'm a vegetarian," I remind her.

"I forgot. Why didn't you say something when I went out to get the food? I could have gotten you something else. I feel bad you're eating that dog food."

"It's not dog food and don't feel bad."

"Have some salad, at least," Cleo says.

"I don't eat bacon."

"Bacos, not bacon. It just looks and smells like bacon."

"It's just that I don't eat anything that looks or smells like bacon."

"But it's not bacon," she insists.

"She won't eat it," Luke says. "Anything that even resembles meat is a four-letter word."

Cleo winks at her son. "Well, that just means more salad for the two of us."

Meanwhile, June Moon breaks into a merciless scream.

"So, Luke, how was your day?" Cleo asks.

"Okay."

"What did you do?" she presses him.

"Not much."

Cleo grows headachy. "Luke, please. Tell me about your day."

"I went to Pier Pressure, then I came home, then I ate bread and water."

"Bread and water?"

"Well, figuratively speaking."

Something much more than a phrase has just passed between Luke and me. We are comrades.

I grin. "Speaking of bread, pass the rolls over here, Luke."

"They're dill," he warns me.

"A little dill won't kill," I say.

AFTER SUPPER my bones want to walk.

"It's getting dark," Cleo says.

"Perfect," I say. Which is true. Cactus Bear comes quickly to me in the night air.

"Look, it's not safe to go walking at night anywhere, even in this neighborhood. There have been purse-snatchings."

This from the woman who used to speed with the top down, dead drunk, bare-breasted, while the rest of the world watched the eleven o'clock news.

"I'll be okay," I say. "Besides, I don't carry a purse."

"If it's practice you want, why don't you hop on the tread-mill?" she suggests.

"I don't do treadmills. My body needs to connect with the

ground and the air and the sky, not a machine. Want to go, Luke?"

"No, thanks," he says, heading up to his room.

S O M E T I M E S   W H E N   I'm walking, the earth speaks to me in a language all its own. It's a tongue only I can hear and interpret. It is telling me that I was born to help people, that the road is my whole laid-out life. And when I'm in that state, I'm rounding the globe in some fantastic dimension bigger than any dream. I will never get tired, I will walk forever, I will help the White Sky build their clinic, and when their spirits are once again healthy, their magic will return to them.

Cactus Bear.

H A L F W A Y   D O W N   the block, I hear Cleo calling after me. I don't slow down—she'll have to catch up, which she does.

"I see you've made some headway," she says.

"Where's June Moon?"

"Still in the highchair. She'll be okay for a few minutes. So what exactly did Luke say today?"

"Nothing deep. But I hope he will."

"Well, what do you think his goddamned problem is?" she says impatiently.

"His *what* problem?"

"Sorry, but I'm just stressed to death here! Do you think he's just going through some adolescent phase?"

"He's going through a phase when he needs his mom."

I hear it loud and clear—her mind is elsewhere.

"Those two dunce brothers, what did you do to straighten them out?" she asks.

"They weren't dunces, they had a learning disability. And I don't think I was much help."

"Yes, yes, you were. By the time you were through with them, they were speed readers."

I think back until I can think no further, until all I see is a strange figure sheathed in fog.

I'm outwalking Cleo, she falls behind, gives up. For one split second I feel sorry for her back there, want to turn around and say all is forgiven, just give me all the old stuff back. But in a breath's time, I come to my senses. There will be no more letting down my guard; there will be no more glimpses of the vulnerable li'l fool who used to dream on. And above all I must remember something: She deserted her family once. And she could easily do it again.

6

MY FATHER left for Dulles Airport on a cool, foggy
early morning. Cleo had been up all night at a Fourth of
July party on the Potomac, but she still drove us, in the Torino,
though she had to be at work at ten. Her eyes were bloodshot
from lack of sleep and smoking pot—even I could tell the difference between a roach and a cigarette butt. Though beauti-
fully strung out, her spirit seemed a little worn.

"Dad, I can't believe you're going to be gone for two months,"
she whined. "I thought the World Bank was going to stop sending you on all these missions in your old age."

My father was amused, in love. "I'm not an old-timer yet,
Cleo."

"No, but you were gone my entire childhood, you know," she
said.

"Mine, too," I said, embracing him from the back seat.

My father basked in this glorious scene, his daughters missing him before he even left the ground.

"I'm just part of the rat race," he said, always fond of American expressions. *Rat race, cog in a wheel, ordinary Joe.* He jotted down such phrases and their meanings in tiny spiral notebooks. Years later I'd find them in drawers all over the house. *Bites one's head off, eat crow, grist for the mill.* Where did he dig them all up? "They hand me an itinerary, I follow it. But two months will go by in a snap. Eight episodes of *The Rockford Files*, and I'll be home. Marcy, you must practice walking faster so you can keep up with me when we resume our walks."

My mother was sulking next to me. "*Rockford Files* all repeats."

My poor mother! She needed my father so much it frightened me to think of her life without him. Her world, like her shoulders, was shrinking before my eyes. But what was it? Was it love for him or fear for herself? When he was gone, his mission projects—planning a highway in Thailand or an airport in Panama City—came second to our running out of rice noodles or seaweed sheets. Our neighbors would gladly drive her to the A&P, but the A&P didn't sell rice noodles or seaweed sheets or the makings for kimchi. And the Korean store was somewhere in Arlington, miles away on some dingy little corner. No way could she navigate anyone there.

"No birthday party for you. You miss birthday," she added.

My father turned around and comforted her in his soft-spoken Korean.

"By time you are home, Cleo already starting school," she scoffed.

Cleo seized up; her eyes froze in the rearview mirror.

"Yah," he said. "Tell you what, Cleo. Marcy and Mommy and me will come for a weekend visit again, okay? We'll walk around the campus, watch the leaves fall, and take you out for a nice prime rib dinner at the Holiday Inn."

"Great," Cleo cracked.

"Bye, Dad."

He took me in his arms and held me as he had so many times before in Dulles Airport. His stubbly chin and the soothing smell of Old Spice come back to me in moments of prayer. I would not let go of him that morning. My heart was roaring louder than the planes over my head.

"Dad, it's too foggy to fly. The pilots won't know where they're going."

"The fog is clearing. Don't worry," he said.

"No, they'll get lost!" I insisted.

"Marcy, be a big girl now," he said in a whisper so low no one else could hear. "Hey, you take care of Mommy, okay? Don't go to the pool every night, she gets lonely. And help her put away the groceries and wash the dishes, she's not a maid."

Time and time again my father would say my mother was a genius who lost direction, while he was a lucky bloke who found his way. What prompted him to say this was his guilt over ending up with the better life. My mother, once a promising young pianist in the city of Sunchun and doted on by her three big brothers, ended up cooking and cleaning in Glover, Virginia, with no one to talk to. Who could have guessed? She was born

into privilege in the north, he was born into poverty in the
south. Her life began as a party, songs and games and celebration in a large household catered to by maids. Chusok was the
grandest celebration, a time of honoring ancestors and celebrating the harvest by feasting on every delicacy known to Koreans.
My mother's favorites were the chestnut-and-black-bean-filled
pastries and the pastel-colored *mochi* rice cakes, which were so
sticky they stuck to her teeth—that was half the fun. War
changed all that. In her flight my mother lost her family and status, while my father made a name for himself as student body
president at Chosun Christian University and later working for
President Rhee. Harvard was on the horizon. As fate would
have it, now their roles seemed reversed. He traveled the globe
first-class while she stayed home, stuck in a world that would
always be a foreign land. Gave up the piano, too.

"*Si tu obtiens un A en français, je t'apporterai un cadeau,*" he
was saying.

"*D'accord,*" I promised, even though he always came home
bearing exotic gifts. Our house was a museum of native dolls in
colorful costumes, primitive sculptures, and decorative plates
that hung on the walls like giant coins. He had also brought me
a nickel ring with my initial on it from Bangkok and a cloth calendar from London.

After he hugged my mother and Cleo, I watched him walk
into the terminal. He was a small man by American standards,
but so distinguished in dress and manner that he stood out in
any crowd. As I did every time I watched him walking away
from us, growing smaller and smaller, I cried out, "Dad!"

He turned around and waved a final good-bye.

. . .

WE DID not take my father for granted. Whether we could
find our way out of Dulles Airport without him was always in
question. We did not feel complete or safe or happy when he was
gone. Our house became empty, a cold, drafty, spiritless place.
Sometimes I would open his closet and press my face against one
of the beloved Hawaiian shirts he had left behind. Whenever he
was gone, I was afraid I would never see him again.

Though moody, my father was more often jovial. Work aside,
he had his own mission: to live a charmed life. Hosting cocktail
parties for three distinct groups of guests—the neighbors, the
World Bankers, and his Korean friends. Reading Tolstoy while
popping cashews into his mouth. Drinking a beer that went down
like heaven on a hot, sweaty Sunday when he was doing yard
work. Playing Korean folk songs on the piano, although his style
was always rusty. Sometimes when he was on a roll he would take
himself too seriously, hit the wrong chord, and shout, "Chum!,"
but mostly he would laugh it off and say, "My two left hands." But
what probably defined his charmed life most of all were his wist-
ful thoughts about retirement on a Hawaiian island.

"Yah, I will sell orchids on the side of the road. Or maybe I
will teach political science at one of the universities. Or both!"

A blue airmail letter from Korea could rip this picture apart.
Cleo knew the details and said I'd never believe how filthy and
lowdown his parents were, those varmints, not in my wildest,
childish dreams. They crowned him a bad first son. How he
shamed them with his greed! How dare he buy Cleo a car when
his mother needed a cosmetic operation on her old, corroded

foot? Soon they would go to their graves not knowing the luxuries they deserved, they complained. Like a nice stone house and food in their bellies wasn't enough? What about the maid and vacations to Inchon?

"Why don't they just do us a favor and lay down and die?" was Cleo's famous line.

My father felt a great duty to live to old age—not for himself, but to take care of his parents, his wife, and his two daughters. He mail-ordered Miracle 50 vitamins that guaranteed *At fifty, you're only halfway there.* And he faithfully took his medicine every day—one blue capsule, one pink pill—for his high blood pressure. Not that I knew what high blood pressure was, but I knew we took walks before supper to fight it. Either that or he had to give up salted fish and kimchi and soy sauce altogether.

"Man does not live on rice alone," he protested.

He bought a stopwatch and we were off. Soon he was walking so fast I took to my skates and eventually my bike. I remember chasing him down the block with the sun setting in my eyes, huffing and puffing.

"Wait up, Dad!"

But he was off like a marathoner running toward a finish line somewhere over the rainbow. Afterward he'd chuckle.

"Forty minutes, seventeen seconds this time, Marcy. Not quite good enough. I'm like an Avis car. I'm number two—I have to try harder."

But try with all his might, it still wasn't good enough. Even Meg's eight ball could predict that his parents would outlive him.

I once overheard Cleo's voice on a winter night when the frost on my window was one *ping* away from shattering:

"Be a bad first son, Dad. Be the baddest first son they've ever set their greedy eyes on. Then maybe you can get some sleep and get on with your life."

WE DROVE home from Dulles Airport, fighting tears. My mother had moved up to the front seat. Her hunched shoulders said it all. The day was suddenly long and hot, with too many hours and nothing to do. After a ten-mile silence on the empty airport access road, Cleo yawned.

"Screw it, I'm calling in sick."

"That bad, bad idea, Cleo," my mother advised her. "Why you think you lost last job? Can't go through life calling in sick. If Daddy do that, we are starving to death."

"I just can't see standing on my feet all day," Cleo said. "I've got to be in a certain funky frame of mind to talk to bongheads all day, and I'm not, Mom."

"What in hell world 'bongheads' mean?" my mother wondered, looking at both of us.

Cleo's sleepy eyes crossed in the rearview mirror. I cracked up and this got my mother going.

We slowly pulled into our driveway, so slowly we're still pulling in there.

NOT LONG after we got home, Cleo dragged herself to her room and passed out, even after a pot of black coffee. My mother sat down at the table and began writing a letter to my father in the morning light. "Frail" would be the word to describe her. If touched, surely her bones would turn to ash.

"I'm going to Tim and Tom's," I informed her.

She didn't stir; she was lost in her letter, and in a light where I was not welcome.

WHAT TIM and Tom needed was more than words to read, I decided. Maybe the words on the page needed more than mechanical meaning. Maybe the words needed heartbeat. If the words had heartbeat, maybe their brains would start ticking.

In those days my favorite book was *To Walk the Sky Path*. It told the gentle story of a Native American boy named Billie who was torn between two worlds—of being an old Indian like his grandfather Abraham or being a new Indian. An old Indian learned by the sights and sounds around him and listened to the voices of his ancestors. A new Indian went to school and listened to his teachers. Even the notion of a clock on the wall was strange to an Indian, who told time by the light in the sky. Billie's grandfather was telling him one thing, his teacher was telling him another. Which world was better? What was his heart telling him while it was being torn in two?

I especially loved Billie's uncle, Mush Jim, for his unbroken will and hushed strength and sad acceptance of his lot in life. The very idea of him warmed me. There were times when I wished he were next to me on the bus, helping me hold my head up high, saying things that would turn my shrinking spine into a strong but angry arrow.

Anyway, the book was a story of deep-rooted meaning that flowed through me like a spring breeze over the river.

Tim was brooding, as usual. If he'd had his way, he would have slammed the book down and run out the door. But he did that yesterday. Today he was trying to scowl me down.

"Walk the sky path? Is that the road to powwow land?"

"Read the first three pages, birdbrain," Tom said, shoving the book in his face. "The sky path is where the wise old Indian goes when he dies. It lights up and leads him to heaven."

"What kind of heaven? Indian heaven?"

Tom thought this concept over very slowly. "I think there's a universal sky path. I think we can all walk there if we're good on earth."

"Do dogs go to heaven?" Tim urgently needed to know. "Will Afro go there?"

MUSH JIM was Jim Mush a couple of times, but all in all, the lesson was a productive one. While their mother drank coffee in the background, we made progress. When Tom was reading, he would stop every few sentences, sometimes stumbling on words, sometimes studying them. The words evoked a universe more stellar than the dry copy of textbooks ever could. Even Tim had marveled over the part when Billie and his big brother Charlie go frogging late into the night—goose bumps rose on his arms. He was right there, on the canoe with them, where life could be defined as nothing more than the earthy sound of frogs croaking in a black swamp.

The lesson ended on a triumphant note. The twins asked if I could leave my book at their house. When I said yes, they high-fived: "Cactus Bear!"

Were they snapped out of their dyslexic state?

WHEN I got back from Tim and Tom's, my mother was still on her letter. So many images defined her, and in all of them she seemed very much alone: Writing a letter, playing Solitaire, stirring over the stove. Anyone near her was invasion from which she ran. A spot check told me she hadn't budged since my departure. Her purse was still on the table next to her pink sweater. Except for her hand moving across a sheet of rice paper, she was paralyzed with grief.

I made myself a bologna sandwich and watched her write in her native script. Her strokes were masterful, foreign. They seemed to burst from her small frame. Except for the occasional English words that popped up—"Marcy," "Cleo," "summer school"—I had no clue what she was writing. At times like this, an Oriental screen went up between us. It divided our lives.

MY FATHER was gone, but after a few days without his middle-of-the-night walking-around sounds we, as usual, with no other choice, came to accept that life went on.

I signed up for French II for the second session of summer school, set on graduating early from Glover High School. It wasn't ambition, just easy math—three years was a quicker death than four. Then I could catch up with Cleo and we could cruise in twin Mustangs around the Beltway and into the horizon. Yeah!

Naturally, whenever I was in public I was on the lookout for Frog Fitzgerald. Obsession had seized me. If I saw him, what would I do? Ignore him? Run away from him? Go into the woods for a smoke with him? And then what? Would he pull some stunt?

Miss Moonface loves me.

THE VERY day I got good news in the mail from Meg—she was moving back from Texas the next month, her father was being transferred back to the Pentagon—Cleo fell ill. It was noon and she was still in bed, cocooned in wet sheets. Her face was oily, her lips dry with fever. Long silver earrings dangled from her earlobes onto the pillow. Her eyelids glittered silvery blue. I had nursed her through hangovers and cramps, but right now she was in the fatal stage of something. She dug her fingernails into my arms and moaned, "I'm sick as a dog, li'l one."

I was freaking out. "Cleo! Should I call an ambulance?"

"No, just let me die in peace. But let me barf up breakfast first."

THE GLOVER-WESTBROOKE Clinic was a small brick building on the edge of town, easily mistaken for a community center or a utility building. There we waited for the results of the test. The waiting room was crowded with teenage girls snapping gum. No one seemed nervous but us. The nurse called Cleo back, and before I even opened a magazine she was heading out the door.

We got into her Mustang and took off. Cleo fidgeted with the radio, searching for a song. "Nowhere Man" came on and she let it play for drama.

"I don't know who the hell the father is. Some dumb bong-head, that's for sure," she spat out.

She turned into a neighborhood and sped down a street of drab white houses.

"Look at those mangy little brats running through the sprinkler—that's how they bathe. Ha! Welcome to Nowhereland, where America dumps their white trash."

"Are you scared?" I wondered.

She ignored me and drove on, deeper into the neighborhood. The roads became narrow and unpaved. A wilderness cluttered with shacks.

"A girl in my school had a baby last year and she never came back. They said when she was giving birth, her hair turned white as a witch!" I said.

Cleo stamped out her cigarette, appalled by the notion of motherhood. "Are you kidding? I'm not having any baby."

I was afraid of what she meant by that. *American Teen* magazine had published pictures of fetuses—miniature babies about to be zapped out of the womb—in an article called "Sex and the Stupid Teen." For weeks I couldn't get those fetuses out of my mind. I saw them everywhere I looked—on my pizza, in my cream of mushroom soup. I felt sick to my stomach.

Cleo was feeling her way out of here; she knew she had gone

too far. She spotted a stop sign and accelerated. She ran it, then a red light. We zipped past gas stations and fast-food joints. We were back in civilization.

"I'm having an abortion," she said without blinking.

"No! You can't let some doctor suck the baby out of you. You can't, Cleo!"

She sighed one final, exasperated sigh, as though she had given up hope on my ever calling her Cleopatra.

"Look, it's not against the law, Marcy. Even Petunias would do it if anyone would sleep with their blubber butts. It's like going to the dentist. Lie down and open wide. Besides, it's not a baby yet, it's just a blob of tissue. Snot!"

She slowed down and came to a halt at a yellow light where Tiki Hut, Hair Haven, and Discount Dry Cleaners intersected.

"Ugh, I just remembered something."

"That it's against your religion?" I asked.

"What religion? My only religion is keeping my wits above water during a downer like this. No, I'm talking about my fortune the other day at the Tiny Tea Cup."

"What did it say?"

"*A gift is on its way,*" she groaned.

MEG WOULD have said that message meant something. That her blob of tissue would grow into a gift, perhaps a gifted child. That it was *not* snot. Meg and I had been best friends since the sixth grade and we could almost read each other's mind.

"Marcy, they only call you Miss Moonface because your face glows like a full moon," she would insist.

"Then why do they call Wanda Gomez 'A Lotta Enchilada'?"

"Because they love enchiladas!"

CLEO FLOPPED in her bed like a sick fish. My mother thought she had come down with the flu from wearing her stone-washed mini-skirt in an air-conditioned store. She spent hours cooking *seol lung tang*—beef bone broth—for Cleo, fretting in Korean. I picked up on "Dr. Choi" and "Torino" and put two and two together: Dr. Choi no longer made house calls, and she couldn't drive Cleo to his office. Cleo swore me to secrecy so I couldn't tell my mother the truth. Lucky for Cleo. If my mother had known Cleo was pregnant, she would have cut her into little pieces and thrown her in the pot.

I think deep down Cleo was petrified of having an abortion, though she compared it to Dr. Choi removing skin tags from my father's neck.

"Snip, snip, that's all it is," she said. "Monday they do their thing, Tuesday I sing."

"Why are you sick, Cleo?" I looked at her stomach, shrunken under a batik midriff. How could a baby be in there? "Does the baby inside of you make you sick?"

"I'm going to self-abort if you keep talking like that!" she cried.

"Sorry."

"Forget it." She calmed down, suddenly stricken with delirium. The room was sweltering from a huge, steamy bowl of *seol lung tang* on her nightstand and Monday was on the dark side of the moon. "Promise me something, li'l one. Don't ever grow up. Whenever you get the urge, open up *Winnie the Pooh* and hide inside the pages. Sneak into Rabbit's home, snuggle up with a quilt, sip tea and honey, and don't fucking ever come out. Don't get messed up with bongheads and Leonard Lewandowskis. They're all scum bums," she mumbled sleepily. "Stick to Mit and Mot and Meg when she gets home. This shit's for the birds. What you're witnessing here is the art of suffering."

A s   C l e o lay suffering in bed, I was suffering, too.

Miss Moonface loves me.

Cleo was in no condition to help me out. And even if she miraculously rose and cornered me into confession, I would never divulge my nickname—I would crawl into a hole and die first.

Miss Moonface loves me.

Meg would know what Frog meant and why he said it. She had a gift of seeing through people and situations—that was her fortune. She said it was a gift given to her by God, by her aunt Luella, who was a mystic in New Mexico, and by an eight ball that never failed. She'd light a candle and fire away. *Will I get an A on my Spanish test? Will Marcy look better with bangs? Will we ever fill out B cups?* The way I saw it, it wasn't the eight ball. It was the hands that held it.

And what hands. That time Meg applied her Magique Mud Masque to my face, all the rotten stuff disappeared like magic. Not because there was magic in the mask. The magic was in Meg's hands.

We had been in the upstairs bathroom—me sitting in a parlor chair, her standing over me. Light from a cathedral window at the top of the staircase flooded the hallway. With one magnificent *voilà*, Meg snapped a towel off the rack and wrapped it around my hair. Then she dipped her fingers into the porcelain jar and brought up green mud.

"Don't move, Marcy. The French say, 'You must suffer to be beautiful.' So suffer and be still for two secs."

"Meg—"

"Don't talk, either. Otherwise I can't spread it on evenly."

"Meg—"

"Shhh!"

I shut up, but reluctantly. I could walk the halls in school all day without one hello, but the minute Meg was within lunging distance it was monologue city. Now I had to sit, not moving, not talking. It was pure torture. Until—

Meg's fingertips spread green mud across my forehead. Now they moved down to my temples, down to my cheeks before slowly, very slowly, spiraling down to my chin. I smelled grapes on her breath from a Diet Faygo she'd been drinking on the bus. Her huge blue eyes, fringed with pale lashes, searched my face not just for missed spots, but for something deeper. My happiness, I bet. Why did Meg care? Why did she hang out with me when she could have her pick of friends? Half the girls on the drill team had strawberry-blond shags like hers—she'd fit in just fine. But no, she'd rather be applying green mud to Miss Moonface. Lucky for me. Her finishing touch along my jaw line was delivered with nothing short of love.

Meg turned on the water to wash her hands, but something shifty-eyed was going on. "Okay, you can talk now."

I tried to, but couldn't. Her Magique Mud Masque had hardened like a giant stone on my face. "Uh," I grunted.

Meg cramped over with laughter, leaning against the iron railing for support as she yelled down the stairs: "Mrs. Moon, get your camera! Let's take a picture of My Favorite Marcy!"

"Nooooo!" I yelled back, feeling my mask crack from cheek to cheek.

My mother disguised her amusement behind her tiny Kodak camera. "What you two goofy girls are doing?"

She snapped our picture and we—two goofy girls—lost our senses, got drunk on our own slapstick shadows, pushing and shoving and tripping each other before rolling onto the carpet in the hallway.

My mother headed back downstairs, shaking her head. "Two goofy girls."

When it was over and we were laid out flat, looking up at the ceiling like we were under some starry spell, I asked Meg, "Why am I your best friend?"

"What do you mean, why? Because you are, that's why!"

"No, I mean, why *me*?"

Inhibition changed our sky, made me wish for five minutes ago, when we were laughing. Or ten minutes ago when my lips were stiff shut. Why did I ever open my big mouth? Everything was ruined. Even between best friends who tried on clothes in the same dressing room, it was easier to keep looking up instead of at each other.

"Because you're funny. And honest. And you let me borrow your clothes whenever I want. And you helped me."

"When?"

"Remember in the sixth grade when I couldn't memorize all the state capitals?"

"Who could?"

"You could."

"Big deal."

"It *was* a big deal, Marcy. I was failing social studies. My cousin Eddie was fine until he flunked one test. One crummy test! After that, he flunked a grade, and after that he just kept flunking. He learned his lesson the hard way: One flunked test will flunk you for life."

"But you never flunked anything."

"Right. Because of you. You helped me memorize all the state capitals by heart, one by one. Remember how we sat on the yellow bench after school? You said you didn't mind taking the late bus home. I got a ninety-six on the test—I mixed up two states."

"The Carolinas?"

"No, the Dakotas. North Dakota—Bismarck. South Dakota—Pierre. I'll never forget those again. Anyway, after I passed that test, I got smarter. Not as smart as you, but smart enough not to flunk anything."

What a dumb thing to say! Meg was much smarter than me. Didn't she know? She could write the "Wonder Girl in the Universe" column with her eyes closed.

SOMETIMES THAT night when Cleo got drunk and said all those things—*mama-san, rice paddies, good old Aunt Bea*— would come back to me like a bad song on the radio and I'd tune it out so fast I couldn't hear it anymore. Not even Meg could have put a positive light on that.

M Y   F I R S T   postcard from my father arrived five days after he left. Like all his postcards, it was oversized. Even then, his words were crammed together to fit all that he had to say. From London, the postcard pictured the Houses of Parliament and the River Thames.

> *My darling Marcy,*
> *I flew in here this morning. From the plane the city was even foggier than when I left you at Dulles Airport. I am always thinking of how concerned you were for your dear old dad. Maybe next year I'll ask McNamara to let me stay home with my younger daughter.*
> *London is rather warm, and the hotel room is rather stuffy. Prices are very high here. The small room I got cost twenty-five pounds (even with the World Bank discount!), which is equal to about fifty dollars. I am flying to New Delhi tomorrow, then the next day to Nepal. Then it's off to Jakarta, Bangkok, Singapore and then I'll swing by Seoul for a couple of weeks to see my parents before returning home on September 7. Of course you will get many more postcards from me by then. Write to me at the Hotel Soaltee Oberoi in Nepal.*
> *Love, Dad*

I ran to my globe and found England, then London. My father seemed in step with the Brits; words like "indeed" and "splendid" came as naturally to him as a tip of the hat.

"If they knew I came from low-class *sangmin* blood they'd kick me back to Korea," he would joke.

My globe was more than a gift or a decoration for my desk. It symbolized who my father was. Where he came from and where he went. He would spin it for me in the dark and our faces would brighten with exploration. Father, daughter, barely breathing, almost touching.

"At night you can light it up, Marcy, and dream of traveling as I did when I was your age. Of course the only globe I had was in my head. But maybe that made the dream bigger, more visible. . . "

Now I pretended he was still here, right next to me, so close I could feel his whiskers brushing my face.

7

ALREADY I miss Cactus Bear, and Pablo. I miss the rustic smell of old wooden things and Pablo's one-eyed way of cruising the aisles. I miss the sound of chimes. Most of all, I miss when we meditate in sync and reach Cactus Bear at the same moment. Nirvana in White Sky.

"Was it a good one?" he'll ask.

"Was it ever," I'll murmur.

I haven't called him, though. I left a message with Ned, the moccasin maker, that I'd be home when I'd be home. That's Pablo's punishment for saying I shouldn't come to San Francisco with a chip on my shoulder, that I have to leave things behind like a trail of smoke. "An immature attitude" were his exact words.

An immature attitude? Cleopatra Moon would have gladly run over a bed of Petunias for a free tube of Poison Boysenberry lip gloss.

The truth is, the *reason* we argued has less to do with Cleo and me than Pablo and me. Pablo wants to help the White Sky, he wants to be married, he wants to adopt a White Sky baby, but most of all he wants my commitment to this life so we can move on.

"Whoa, there," I'm always saying.

And this frustrates him almost as much as his past life as a tax attorney. But has he truly left that life? If he swore to it, I'd commit forever. But I'm no beggar. Love is, or isn't.

Still, I miss Pablo and Cactus Bear.

It's not the five-day absence per se. I could sleep a week in White Sky and wake up ready to brush away cobwebs and tag woven blankets. I could walk for a month in the desert without a drop of water and find contentment. But five days in San Francisco and I'm light-years from home, can't imagine walking through the front door of Cactus Bear, going upstairs, and finding Pablo eating breakfast all alone, checking the clock and calendar. Is that what he's doing this very moment while I'm in Cleo's kitchen waiting for my tea to cool?

Cleo sweeps past me in a crisp white linen suit.

"Countdown to the Global Gourmet Food Show. This Sunday a star is born!"

Being a star is fundamentally Cleo. Abandoning the ones she loves might be a fairly apt description, too.

"Anyway," she's yapping, "I have to set up the booth on Saturday, so I'll be leaving Friday. Do you think you're ready to handle the kids by yourself for five days?"

"In the name of the White Sky tribe, yes," I say.

Cleo sits down at the table with me, a natural beauty to behold in the morning light. Not her or me—I mean the table with its nicks and coffee rings. I dig its character in a million-dollar home. Cleo wanted to throw the monstrosity out, but it was Stu's from his Brooklyn days and it was the one thing he couldn't let go.

"Marcy," she says half-humorously, "who the hell are you?"

"Cleo, the only way I can answer you is that I am who I am and that's all who I am."

"No, not good enough. Who is Marcy Moon circa right now, right here, in my house. And answer me in English, not in Pop-eye Zen."

"No matter where I am, I am many things."

"See? See what I mean?"

"What? I don't get it," I say.

"Everything you say, everything you do, goes against the main grain."

"I take that as a compliment."

"Well, don't. Or do! All I'm saying is that there's unique and there's weird. I'm trying to figure out which one you are."

"If walking instead of driving is weird, call me a weirdo."

"Are you trying to tell me you don't drive?"

"Not anymore."

"How do you get around?"

"I walk. I'm in a walking mode for life."

Cleo digests this as if she just swallowed an elephant whole. "Marcy, let's talk about this Moccathon."

"It's a week from tomorrow, noontime till the end of time."

"You're doing it again. Look, I know you're going to walk your heart out, but you're not going to walk forever. At some point

you're not going to be able to go any farther. Do yourself a favor
and accept it. If you only go five miles, it won't be the end of the
world."

"Yes, it will be, Cleo. It will be the end of the White Sky
world."

"Good grief, Marcy, are you serious? You are, aren't you?"

I HAVE this urge, this need, this calling, to walk far. But
what I'm walking toward is still a mystery to me. Walk forever?
Just the thought of it has got me spinning in heaven. It will
take me to the other side of the world.

LUKE LEFT before breakfast, so June Moon and I spend
most of the day alone. A bowl of oatmeal wouldn't keep him
here, nor would my company. A minor setback. Like when we
wait for someone to come into Cactus Bear and take a cracked
vase off our hands, patience pays off.

While I spoon applesauce into June Moon's mouth, I am
feeding her soul. Her moist lips speak to me and I hold her
closer. I love the warm, blanketed feel of her body, her tiny
heart beating through it. I love her essence and being which
are as pure as Cleo's are tainted. I love her. I should wrap her
up in my arms and steal her away to White Sky, where her future will be securely bundled up in my arms and sleep will
come soon.

But for now June Moon watches me slice and dice potatoes,
carrots, celery stalks. I'm here for seven more days—why not

make a soup that will last the visit? By next Wednesday it will be stew, and I'll have one last bowl to fortify me for my walk.

I cook my soup long and slow, through more feedings and naps.

CLEO CALLS, says she won't be home for supper. The plant's in chaos, the office has been declared a disaster area.

"If I make it through the day, it'll be a miracle," she moans.

And if she doesn't make it, can I keep June Moon?

LUKE STIRS his soup with hopelessness. "Where's the beef?"

"In the freezer," I reply.

He sighs, takes a few spoonfuls, gives up.

"Not hungry?" I ask.

"Not anymore."

"If you washed all the additives and preservatives and sauces and animals out of your system, you'd worship this soup."

"How do you eat it?" he wonders.

"One spoonful at a time."

To my surprise, Luke laughs. It's music, pure music!

I seize the moment.

"Luke, you and I have all these choppy sentences going back and forth, but what we need is one long run-on sentence. Pablo and I play something we call Expression. It's a game where we alternate talking for three minutes nonstop. The object of Expression is to see how long we can go at it. Fifteen minutes, two hours. Once we went at it all night. The next day we didn't have anything to say to each other until lunch. Which was okay, be-cause there's something to be said for silence, too."

"Who's Pablo?"

"My companion."

"Does that mean he's your boyfriend?"

"Yes, I guess so."

"Where is he?"

"He's back in White Sky, minding Cactus Bear."

"You work together?"

"We work together, we live together, and we make soup to-gether," I say.

"Does he like it? The soup, I mean?"

"Soup is his savior. You have to understand, he was a worka-holic, gassed on black coffee, wracked with ulcers and panic at-tacks, ready to call it a day every day. But he didn't, not even when a power client poked his right eye with a Waterman pen and blinded him."

"He's blind?"

"In one eye he is. The last straw came when he was too crip-pled with stress to drive anymore. He could barely bend to get into a cab. Being half-blind, he asked me out for coffee, then asked me if I wanted to start a new life with a stranger. At the time my life revolved around an unfulfilling job at an organic shop called Soul Food and a mother who had more fun with her Korean friends than me. So I said, why not? Now he likes herbal tea, me, and reaching Cactus Bear."

"Does he like just you?" Luke mumbles. "Or does he have someone else, like Stu did?"

"What did you say, Luke?"

He frowns, taking it all back. "Nothing."

An awkward pause follows. I know what he said, and he knows what I heard. An alarm goes off in my head. But now is not dwelling time, or he'll close up forever.

"Luke, let's play Expression!"

"What's the point of playing?"

"To get into each other's head. To have fun!"

"What does the winner get?"

"There is no winner."

"But I can't talk for three minutes," he argues.

"Try it. Talk about anything. School. Sports. My soup. Anything."

"I don't want to," he says.

"Then I'll go first," I say. "When I was your age I had a best friend by the name of Meg Campbell. She was a small girl with strawberry-blond hair. We were outcasts in school—me because I was different, she because I was her best friend. This was the seventies; I was the only foreigner in school. Years later we would go our separate ways, but in junior high, pliers couldn't pull us apart.

"Somehow we got it in our heads that we were going to write what we called the Song of the Century. It would be the song that would lift us from our measly lives in Glover, Virginia. It would elevate us to cult status, or at least make us popular. It would blare across radio stations and stay in the Top Forty forever. We called ourselves the M&Ms. Nothing calmed the adolescent fires more than our singing together. Our harmonizing defined who we were, together, forever, the M&Ms. I remember the first song we wrote. We called it

'Why Am I Always Waiting?' The lyrics were somber but the tune was pure pop.

Why am I always waiting?
Are the dreams I dream for real?
My mind is now debating
Over images I feel.

"My dad liked this song. He would sing it in the shower and in the car on the way home from work. He said the song made him feel good, got him going on his walks. I could never keep up with him, but I could tell when he was singing by the back of his head. It was a happy head. I wonder if he was just singing the song to make me feel good. He was that way. I remember one wintry morning his eyeglasses got fogged up and he purposely kept walking with them that way just to make me crack up."

Luke buzzes too quickly. "Your three minutes are up."

"Okay," I say doubtfully. "Now it's your turn."

"I told you. I can't talk for three minutes."

"Then why don't we start with one minute. Can you do that?"

"I don't want to. Not right now."

"Maybe another time."

"So this man you're talking about. He's my grandfather?"

STU HAD been having an affair. The bald guy with a humble hello fooled everyone. But did he fool Cleo? Oh, I can just picture her face at the moment of discovery. Her Cleopatra eyes—after all these years—magically reappeared as bold and dramatic as ever. And behind the eyes, the deadly anger. And behind the deadly anger...

Her darkness, wanting out.

And I can just picture Cleo losing her cool in the car that night with Stu, arms flailing.

You bastard, I could kill you for doing this to me!

Cleo, let me explain, for God's sake!

Explain it to the devil instead!

The car swerves off the road, Cleo grabs the wheel, as crazed as she was one summer afternoon in 1976.

I'M CRADLING June Moon in an easy chair, daydreaming we're in White Sky when a whiff of wretched perfume stuns me. Cleo stands over me, it's past midnight.

"Sorry I'm so late."

My eyes hush her.

"Everything go okay with Luke tonight?" she whispers.

I nod.

"What did you two do?"

"Play Expression," I whisper back.

A GAME of Expression would be telling right now. Cleo's suit is wrinkled, her hair is a disgraceful mess. Who has she been with tonight, Bob, Sid, or Elliot?

God help all the doomed men who have loved Cleo!

8

OWEN BEAN lived and breathed for that one moment when Cleo would notice him, nod, and go for a stroll with him. If it was a starry night and chance was in the air, a tender first kiss was a possible dream. And from that, the whole suburban works. Dating, marriage, kids.

But Cleo didn't know he was alive. The mere mention of his name made her yawn. Owen who?

Oh.

He was Cleo's age, although they seemed generations apart. His hair was crew-cuttish and his jeans looked pressed even when he was washing his blue Camaro. His parents owned Bean Cleaners, but business was off, what with Discount Dry Cleaners popping up all over town. Like his younger sister Jennifer, Owen worked at the cleaners part-time in between his classes at the community college. Our families were politely acquainted.

My father would wave. "Hello, Martin."

Mr. Bean would wave back. "Hello, Bok Young."

"How is business?"

"Dry."

Whenever my father was overseas, Owen would mow our lawn, no charge. That was the magic of Cleo.

"So," he said, bagging grass, "where's Cleo these days? Her car's here."

"She's sick," I said, helping him.

"Nothing serious, I hope."

"She'll be okay by Tuesday."

Owen grinned. "What's Tuesday?"

"The day she'll be feeling better," I said, without further explanation.

If I told him Cleo was pregnant, he'd have a cow. Probably stop mowing our lawn, too.

Thankfully, he dropped the subject of Cleo for now with a survey of our yard.

"Your dad did a good job with the brick walkway, Marcy."

"I helped him. We all did," I said.

Our weekend projects were famous on Wandering Lane. Widening the driveway so Cleo's Mustang could park next to the Torino, laying stones for a new and improved patio.

"My job was taking up the bricks from the back yard."

"They were part of your old patio."

"Yeah, and then I hosed them off and carted them to the front yard in a wheelbarrow."

Big deal, my job—no doubt Owen was summoning up the sight of Cleo in her cutoffs and garden gloves, doing nothing.

He nodded. "I remember. And I like the garden your dad recently built on the side of the lawn, with the rocks and junipers. Only problem is, the garden is located where the lawn dips. After a few days of heavy rain in a row, I'm afraid the garden will turn into a marsh."

My mother's voice sneaked up behind us.

"What turn to marshmallow?"

Owen put his arm around her. "Perfectly put, Mama Moon. Your garden will turn into one giant, soggy marshmallow."

"We need drain, I keep on telling husband ground too wet there. Rain makes flood. Right, Owen?"

"Right on."

"Owen, how family business?" she asked him, concerned. Besides Meg, Owen was about the only outsider my mother was comfortable with, broken English and all. "Your daddy work too hard. Your mommy, too. Seven days a week."

Owen sighed. "Let me put it this way. 'Wash 'n' Wear' is a dirty word in our household."

FROM NOON to nightfall, Owen worked on the side of our yard, digging a tunnel for the drain. With each lump of dirt he shoveled onto the wheelbarrow, he was hoping Cleo would come out that door.

WHENEVER I would check on Cleo I would crave the lipsticks in the wooden cigar box and the endless knots of slinky things in her drawer. My arms ached to rip off my smock top.

My feet were dying to kick off my moccasins and bury them in the back yard, those worn little critters. Last year Meg and I went to Miles of Styles and walked out with identical moccasins. How juvenile that seemed now.

When would Monday come so that Tuesday Cleo could sing and I could do my thing?

MONDAY CAME in the form of thunder and lightning and downpour. Meg would say it was the wrath of God causing havoc. That, or Cleo's subconscious.

Owen had to abandon his drainage project for the day. He had already dug out the whole tunnel, now he was lining it with tiny stones. From my window I watched him trudge away in the mud, defeated. I liked Owen, even though it wasn't me he loved. He would make a good boyfriend but he wasn't Cleo's type.

"He's a dry, clean bean!"

"He starches his underwear!"

"His ROTC 'do drives me nuts!"

As it was, Owen could dig up gold and Cleo would see mud. So him trudging away under a dismal sky is how I most remember him.

I had to cancel my lesson with Tim and Tom to accompany Cleo to the clinic—we told my mother we were going to Dr. Choi's. She grabbed her raincoat and began frantically hunting for an umbrella.

"I come," she said. "Marcy! Find umbrella! Maybe in basement by back door!"

"No!" Cleo reacted. "The weather's bad. Stay in and make me more *seol lung tang*. Please, Mom?"

My mother squeezed her raincoat, crushed. On the most basic level, she could not be part of her daughters' lives. Once she gave birth to us, but now she could not interpret our songs, thoughts, or secrets.

C L E O   W A S in a hushed mood, driving with military precision in the rain. The gusto in her gear-shifting had gone down the sewer. She wore a baggy white blouse and a black skirt, easy to remove. She wasn't smoking—even the ashtray fumes made her gag. No radio, no guys going wacko. It was a gray, glum, hopeless day.

"When this is all over I'm taking you to Satisfaction, li'l one. Shop till you drop. On me." She paused as though an unspeakable loneliness had caught up with her.

When Cleo was sixteen, all her girlfriends snubbed her. Dumped her like a bag of trash, she told me. She looked around for a behind-the-wheel partner and—*vroom!*—they were gone. Like her looks, it happened overnight. Before, there were slumber parties and talking on the telephone until midnight. Now that her hair moved like the ocean when she walked, they wouldn't be seen with her for all the free pepperoni pizza in Mario's. Cleo said she didn't give a flying four-letter word for all those waltzing Petunias, but I was beginning to wonder.

.   .   .

WE WALKED out of the rain and into the clinic. All eyes were on Cleo, even in her dowdy outfit. We sat off to ourselves in a corner and waited. The waiting room was too cold; my teeth began to chatter. Cleo's jaw was jittery, her face ashen. She looked ready to self-abort. Finally, her name was called by a red-haired nurse who dwarfed her as they headed down a hallway.

I WAITED by myself. My damp clothes froze on my skin. My soul turned to ice. Someone turned down the air conditioning and within minutes the room stank of deodorant and hair spray. I hated this place more than a Texaco bathroom.

Girls breezed in and out. Most of them had boyfriends waiting for them and this made me sad for Cleo. Where were all her boyfriends? She had more than could fill this crummy clinic.

"Marcy Moon," I heard.

A nurse led me past closed doors until we came upon Cleo in a room behind a half-opened door. She was sitting up, braving a smile. Her Barbie-doll legs dangled from the examining table.

"Hey, li'l one. It's over."

"Did it hurt?" I asked her.

"To high heaven. The doctor kept poking and poking at me like I was some damn campfire. Some of the nurses are pissed I didn't dance out of here on my tippy-toes like their other Petunia patients. Well, I'm sorry, I don't open up like the Grand Canyon."

"Can we go home now? I don't like it here."

"Promise me you'll never have sex. Never, never, never. Not even if the school hunk falls all over you, risks his life for you, tattoos your face on his left ball for you. Never! Better to be a nun or a dyke or a neutered bitch. If you ever want to get poked, just remember this: raw ground round."

"Can we go home now?" I repeated. "Mom might worry and call Dr. Choi."

"Patience, li'l one, I'm still recuping. I'm not sure I can drive yet. Nurse Yanofsky—the gentle giantess—told me to hang out till I've got some more color in my face." Her voice cracked. "She held my hand through the whole nightmare, can you believe it?"

I whined until Cleo slowly and unsteadily got to her feet.

"I think I'm okay now," she said.

But she wasn't. Blood gushed from between her legs and onto the floor.

"Cleo, you're bleeding!" I screamed.

She stuffed a towel between her legs, but it did no good. She fell to her knees.

"Marcy, go get me help."

I FOUND Nurse Yanofsky lining up urine samples on a tray.

"Please help me!" I cried.

"What's wrong, honey?"

"My sister's bleeding to death!"

She dropped what she was doing—literally—and rushed to Cleo's aid.

THE DOCTOR said it was nothing. He was in and out so fast all I saw was a white coat.

Cleo and I waited in the room for her skirt to be washed and dried. She was braving that smile again, not saying much. Was she sedated or in shock? Nurse Yanofsky checked in on Cleo twice. Each time Cleo twitched as though she wanted to say something more than thanks but couldn't find the words. Eventually, another nurse came in and threw Cleo's skirt at her. Like half the world, she despised Cleo and her dolled-up Cleopatra eyes.

Cleo quietly got dressed.

THE NEXT day was so blue and summery that the day before was a distant memory. Cleo made a miraculous recovery, woke up shining. I was helping Owen lay a long rubber pipe in the tunnel when she bounced out of the house to take me shopping, as promised.

"Feeling better?" he asked Cleo.

She flashed her pearly whites in a horribly cold fashion and replied, "Feeling fantastic." He started to say something more but she cut him off by rattling her key chains at me. "Hustle, li'l one, I've got to be at work by two."

En route to the mall Cleo dove into a monologue about how some guys she knew had been busted at the cabin the weekend before. Earrings torn from earlobes, heads scalped, and enough bricks to build a house confiscated from a closet. She ended with: "Being sick in bed was a blessing in disguise. Otherwise, I'd be behind bars right now."

"He likes you, Cleo."

"Who?"

"Owen."

"Pop open the Champagne!"

"Know why he's been working in our yard?"

"No, and I don't want to, *merci*."

"He's digging a drain so the rainwater will flow into the street instead of flooding our garden."

"Oh, no, wrinkled clothes!"

"It's nice of him to do that, don't you think?" I continued. "He wouldn't do it for just any old neighbor. I mean, it's a lot of work."

"Drop it, Marcy."

"The whole time you were sick he was out there digging and sweating up a storm. Mom was afraid he was going to get dehydrated like me when I threw up spaghetti and she had to call Dr. Choi, so she kept bringing him out iced tea after iced tea until he finally admitted he didn't like iced tea. But he didn't say a word for the longest time because he's so polite."

Cleo put her foot down, floored it, and screeched, "One more word about Owen and you're out the door! I mean it, Marcy, you can just hitchhike home!"

"Sorry," I said.

"Look, it's just that you all act like he's some saint! Well, he ain't! Okay?"

"Okay."

EVERY DAY I was becoming more aware of Cleo's secret self that made itself known in blurts—her Petunia calling, her hissing out of nowhere over something trivial that had happened years ago, something so seemingly minuscule how could she remember it? A grocery clerk who failed to say thank you. The teller who closed the drive-up window on her—at closing hour. This. I'd seen it head-on that one night, and I was in no hurry to see it again. Even as she cooled down and eased up on the pedal, I kept my mouth shut.

CLEO'S STRAPPY sandals clicked on the tiles and woke up Town Hall Mall. Every guy—at Cookie's 'n' Milk, at Sonny's Shoe Shine, at the key kiosk—looked up, then stopped in mid-motion. It was modern-day Pompeii.

We got to Satisfaction. The music of Jimi Hendrix was her calling, and she boogied on in. She was totally at home here, flipping through a stack of glittery black T-shirts. A skinny salesman with frizzy albino hair snaked up to her and hugged her from behind.

"Cleopatra!"

"Hey!" she replied.

The two engaged in some kind of lewd ritual, rubbing each other's body parts in sync with a guitar solo. Still in the doorway, I watched. For years Meg and I had strolled by Satisfaction with its leather displays and strobe lights, wishing we could be a part of the older, funky scene but knowing it was off limits to teenyboppers like us. Now here I was, being waved in by Queen Cleo.

"Marcy"—Cleo beckoned me with a black leather belt —"get your li'l bod in here."

"Who was that guy?" I asked her.

"Who knows or cares?" she said, eyeing a sale rack of sheer blouses. "But whoever he is, he said he would give me a great discount."

AFTER AN hour-long hunt I squeezed into a pair of designer jeans so tight they bruised me as I zipped up in the dressing room. The Grateful Dead blared out of a speaker over my head as I sized myself up in the mirror and strutted my stuff. Not bad for a ne'er-been-kissed girl. Not bad, period. Cleo split open the curtain and caught me in the act.

"What do you have on?"

"Just jeans," I said.

"Just jeans? Try X-rated jeans. Try hooker jeans. Try get-arrested-for-being-an-underaged-slut jeans. You must be out of your ever-loving mind if you think I'm buying you those. Dad would have my head and Mom would mount it. Here," she said, holding up a bunch of smock tops on hangers.

Crushed, I took the jeans off—no easy feat—and tried on smock top after smock top.

"Li'l one, you're so adorable!" Cleo squealed.

The one I got—the one Cleo picked—was yellow with tiny buttercups all over it.

CLEO STEERED me toward Subs, Etc. for a quick bite. Actually, she just drank Tab and smoked, sensing my disappointment while I chewed on a giant slice of pepperoni pizza— and the image of me in those jeans. The way they were so snug in the butt, the way they cut a perfect bell. The cool, faded feel. The black silver-buckled belt that gleamed with authority as I turned this way and that in the dressing-room mirror. Imagine me in the sun, standing on a rock. I could beat up any jackass with one bitchy look.

"You don't need to show off your bod, Marcy," Cleo preached. "You're too smart for that. First it's a shoulder, then a thigh—in the eyes of guys you're just a walking crotch. Someone like you shouldn't dress for Mit and Mot mentalities."

"Tim and Tom aren't like that," I said defensively.

"I'm not talking about Mit and Mot per se. I'm talking about the generic dumbshit state of men."

"The what?"

She choked on her Tab and stamped out her cigarette, so exasperated. "Don't be stupid, li'l cupid. Show off your brains, not your bod. Otherwise, you'll end up with an ignoramus anus."

"I'm not brainy," I argued.

"Says who?"

"Says me!"

"You're breezing through advanced French, *ma cherie!*"

"No, I'm not!"

"Fine. Who can beat you at Omok?"

I picked at a piece of pepperoni, wondering what Omok had to do with me in those jeans.

"No one! That's who!" Cleo said. "Not even old Gramps! Village champ since the turn of the century. You murdered him, game after game, while he sat there stroking his decrepit old chin, mumbling in Korean. Dad was trying so hard to control himself his whole face turned beet red. Mom had to leave the room; she knew what would come down if she started laughing. Death by Grandma's breath. Here you were, a punk, whipping his ass with your eyes closed. How old were you? Five? Six?"

I was ten, actually. The day I learned how to play Omok, the monsoon rains were falling with no end in sight. Which was bad news for Cleo and me. The rain had gone on for the third or fourth day in a row. The only place we could flee our grandmother's wrath—her maid-beating, her cursing her own ugly bunions—was on the roof. It was big and flat, railed off by a rusty fence we wouldn't touch for fear of tetanus or leprosy. From here the village rose before us. The seedy bathhouse with its blinking lights, the noodle boys delivering big, hot, cheap bowls of *jajamein* by cart for four hundred won—fifteen cents—to mud dwellings. It was nice up there, less urine in the air. But on rainy days we were trapped inside. No escape.

A limo was waiting for my father outside the gates. He always had secret business meetings in Seoul, all day long. Today my mother was going with him, to meet a distant cousin in town who had also fled from North Korea, for an afternoon of commiseration. I remember he was bald from using some strange hair tonic. On their way out, my father set out a game table for Cleo and me, called a Paduk table. It was used for many Korean games, including the famous game of Omok. He rushed over the rules, checking his watch.

"I don't get it, Dad," I whined. "Stay and play a few games with us."

"You two genius girls will figure it out," he said.

We felt our way through the game on the small wooden table with its black grid pattern painted on the top. Two matching bowls contained polished stones, black ones and white ones. Traditionally, the older player—Cleo, in this case—has the honor of using the white stones. The object of the game is to get five stones in a row before being blocked by the opponent's stones. It's a simple game of strategy that can go off the board with a good opponent, which Cleo was not. She was distracted by our grandmother, who faked a gold-toothed smile as she squatted down to watch us play.

"She looks like an old hen about to lay an egg," Cleo muttered. "Hag!"

We played for hours, until Cleo gave up and began rereading letters from Bobbi, her best friend back home.

That night, as the monsoon rains continued their downpour, my grandfather, who had heard I'd been creaming Cleo all day, challenged me to a game.

"Play," he said.

Everyone—my parents and assorted relatives whose names I never knew—gathered around the table. When my grandfather played Omok, it was an event. The Almighty Il Young Moon was going to take someone down. From his bamboo mat of a throne he sat cross-legged, juggling his superior white stones from palm to palm. My father watched me with a sympathetic eye, knowing I didn't have a competitive bone in my body. Marcy Moon was prepared to die without shame. I was, after all, only ten. The whole time Cleo was cheering on the sidelines, "Kick his arthritic butt!"

My grandfather mistakenly bargained on a pattern I had mastered that morning: creating two intersecting rows of three stones. This would be instant death, because an opponent can only block one end in one move. With the other end open, a row of four stones can be created. The opponent has no choice but to block that end. With the next turn, an open-ended four-stone row with the other row can then be created. At this point, the opponent can't possibly block both ends in one move—and suffers defeat. But I blocked my grandfather before he could ever create two intersecting rows of threes. And I kept blocking him. Each time I did he grunted in Korean. And when I beat him effortlessly, he cried, *"Aigoo!"*

And then, "Again! Play!"

We played for hours. Each and every time I won. When he gave up with a final grunt, he was white and pasty as a boiled *mandu* dumpling. That was Cleo's description. By now my father was in the background drinking Korean beer and eating peanuts. It was his way of celebrating.

"My Marcy is a genius," he must have said a hundred times on our Northwest Orient flight bound for Honolulu. "She creamed him."

A week later, on our way home from Friendship Airport, he stopped at the Korean store and bought me my own Paduk board.

WHEN CLEO dropped me off at home there was a postcard waiting for me. It was postmarked New Delhi, India, and pictured the Taj Mahal against a stunning turquoise sky.

My darling Marcy,
It is nearly thirty years since I last set foot on Indian soil. Of course that is not counting stops at airports. In 1948, that is

fourteen years before you were born, and when I was still a student, I landed in Calcutta and traveled to Madras by train. That time I did not have much money in my pocket. Much less even than you have now that you are earning all that tutoring money. I am so proud of you for being a smart girl and for donating half your earnings to Peace of Mind Charity. Those Appalachian kids are in the same boat as your poor pop was some years ago. My first "real" pair of shoes were sneakers from Goodwill.

I hope by now you are writing to me at the Jakarta Hilton.

Love, Dad

P.S. I forgot to send the book order to the Book-of-the-Month Club. Do you remember the brochure I showed you? That is on the rec room table. Order the book you like and do the same if the brochure for the next month arrives. We shouldn't get the books we don't want.

I went directly to my room, shut the door, turned on the globe on my desk. India lit up like the Taj Mahal at night. How many miles away was my father when he wrote this? Ten thousand miles, I calculated. And what was he doing when he wrote it? Eating breakfast in his room? What did he eat? Curried eggs? Did he take his Miracle 50 vitamin?

I had no idea where he was this very second, no idea what he was doing. He could spin off the globe and into the unknown and how would I know?

My mother cracked open the door.

"Marcy, what you are doing?"

"Looking at India," I said. "Come in."

She stood over me. "India a very big place. So hot. Too many people. Stinks sometimes. Like Korea in summertime."

"You've been to India?"

"Daddy told me."

"Mom, why was he in India when he was a student? How could he afford to go there?"

"When he a student at Chosun Christian University, he picked to represent South Korea in Asian Student Christian Federal Conference in Ceylon," she said deliberately from memory. "Only one delegate picked from whole country. Your daddy."

"Wow." I nodded, still fixated on my globe. "Where is he now, Mom? Right now."

She moved the globe, slowly navigating herself with her index finger. It traced over India, the Indian Ocean, then gently landed in Indonesia. "He arrive at Jakarta Hilton yesterday. Man at front desk give him our letters waiting for him. Daddy always like that."

Something welled up in me, something so urgent my teeth were chattering. I swung around to her.

"Mom, I didn't write to Dad in Indonesia yet! I didn't have time! What am I going to do? There wasn't a letter from me waiting at the front desk!"

"Daddy know you busy girl, tutor every day, take French. Beside, Cleo and I both write. She write three letters last week."

"But she was sick."

"She write from bed."

I was a bad daughter. A worthless daughter. Cleo wrote three letters from her deathbed while I was thinking about her clothes in the closet, the way my breasts pointed out of her purple halter. About Frog Fitzgerald. How could I?

"I wanted to write, Mom. I wanted to write to him!"

"So you write him now."

"No, I have to call him. Right now!"

"Long-distance too expensive. We not the Kennedys."

"But I'll pay for it. I have the money!"

"It now two in morning in Jakarta. Daddy hear your voice and have a heart attack. Think I am dead. No, Marcy."

BY THE light of my globe I wrote my father a long letter. Again, his presence materialized next to me, examining the continents with his lonely eyes. My letter was mostly about Owen and the drain, about my mother and I tracing his whereabouts on my globe, about Tim and Tom, about how much money I had earned to date, and how much I had sent to Peace of Mind Charity. No mention of Cleo and her messy abortion or me in Satisfaction. These were not the daughters he thought of in his fond, quiet moments, in hotel restaurants, or on an airplane, looking down for us, dots on a map, so many miles away.

9

NOT THAT I think a cheating husband deserves a shrine, but Stu has just left this world and already his earthly possessions seem to have left, too. A couple of weeks ago he was probably shuffling around in silk pajamas, now there's hardly a trace of him. Just golf clubs in the closet and, bizarrely, a shot of his jacketed torso in June Moon's formal christening portrait. Cleo and Luke are sitting with June Moon, all smiles, but Stu is standing up, head cropped.

If it weren't for my phone phobia, I'd call Cleo at the office and casually inquire as to the whereabouts of Stu's stuff. Just to feel her out, just to hear the tone in her voice. I'm suspicious. I wait for her check-in call.

"Stu was a minimalist," Cleo explains. "If he didn't need it at his fingertips, it went into files or storage. Clutter fuzzed the bottom line."

Mr. Money, that's the image Cleo's selling, but I'm not buying it. That's not the Stu I saw. We met only once, at the Hanguk Home for my mother's sixty-fifth birthday, and he seemed more interested in the Korean buffet than his cell phone, which he turned off.

"And he refused to have any pictures of himself in the house," she further explains. "He saw himself as just another bald Jewish guy. Can you figure that?"

I figure Cleo is calling him that out of revenge.

"Marcy, why are you so concerned about Stu's things?"

"I'm just concerned that there's no mourning period going on here. No one's shedding any tears. It feels unnatural and unhealthy."

"Look, Marcy, I loved my husband, but I don't have time to bawl like a baby. And I'm not going to feel guilty about it. Stu would consider a mourning period like Sundays: precious time wasted, Wall Street's closed. Anyway, I've got to go. Can you hear all the commotion in the background? We're trying to get ready for the show but we're still in production, filling orders. It's a zoo! I can't stop, not for one self-pitying minute or I'll go under like the *Titanic*." She hangs up.

It's that notion of love again that bothers me. She loved us all but in the end of every story there's only Cleo.

J U N E   M O O N and I are just getting to know each other. She is always warm and beautiful, her lips are always wet, just kissed. I could hold her forever, out on the porch with

Pablo, drinking iced herbal tea and watching the Nevada sun go down.

And Luke I could love in a heartbeat if he would let me close enough to hear it. In White Sky he would let his guard down, give up Suicide Spell for the sight of dawn breaking over the desert. In White Sky he would give me more than one-liners; the poetry of dusk would inspire him to speak all night long.

E V E R Y   D A Y Luke comes home earlier from Pier Pressure. An encouraging sign, I think.

"Luke, take a walk with June Moon and me," I suggest. "We'll grab some lunch. What do you say?"

"Okay," he says as though a little enthusiasm would kill him.

He kicks an invisible stone all the way up the street, around the corner, and onto an uphill block of small shops. I tell him all about the ancient White Sky, how they could turn arrows into lightning and make rain. But their isolation destroyed them, their spirits grew sick, their magic disappeared. Now they need an herbal healing clinic to help restore themselves. Hence, the Moccathon. Luke sighs with lack of interest.

"Luke, does it bother you that you don't know your natural father?"

"No."

"Are you mad that your mom married Stu and not him?"

His profile hardens. "No."

"Okay," I say. "Let's go around the block one more time before lunch. I'll just close my eyes and pretend I'm at my Moc-cathon."

His face brightens. "Don't bump into any cactus."

"I just got a great idea, Luke. Why don't you be my partner in the Moccathon? Together we can begin the healing process for the White Sky! Together we can save them from extinction!"

"My mom wouldn't even let me go to a Fourth of July concert in Union Square," he recalls glumly.

But what if she didn't know?

WE STEER into Bayside Gourmet. Luke gets juice while I pick up a bag of lentils, a carton of soy milk, and some organic oranges. We pass an aisle stocked with Cleo's Creations in countless varieties. How much sauce does the world really need? A moot question—Cleo's face could sell bottled birdshit. While I'm waiting in line, a screeching voice behind me sends years of meditation down the drain.

"Oh, my God, it's her!"

I turn around. A skinny, tanned woman with crinkly lips is holding up a bottle of Poppy Pepper Corn Sauce in my face.

"It's you! Cleo!"

"No, ma'am," I say.

She examines me with telescopic eyes. "But you look exactly like her!"

June Moon stirs awake in a glare of fluorescent lights.

"It's not me," I insist.

.   .   .

WHO COULD mistake us? There's Cleo, a woman with bronze-dusted cheekbones and smoky kohl eyes. And then there's me, without even a mole for décor.

"You sort of look alike," Luke says, matter-of-factly, "because you're sisters."

WE STOP for lunch at the Umbrella Cafe. Luke orders pizza, I order the veggie dip and whole-wheat chip platter. Too casually, he says, "Tell me more about your dad."

"Your grandfather," I say.

"Yeah, whatever. You can do the Expression thing if you want."

So I begin. "My father traveled all the time for his job. I knew he was getting important things done, but I didn't care; I just wanted him home. He wrote me every day from overseas but sometimes his handwriting was hard to read. He had so much to say he would squeeze it all on one postcard. It was as if he was always in a hurry to get a thousand things done at once and couldn't keep up with his racing mind.

"Anyway, I must have been whining about his absence because for my tenth birthday he bought me a globe that lit up with a switch. He said that whenever he was gone I could just turn on my globe and find where he was and know that he was thinking about me, maybe even writing me a postcard that very minute. The truth is, whenever I was looking at my globe, he was asleep, not writing postcards. That's how far away he was, in another time zone. Even now I like to think that he's just in another time zone, that someday we'll meet again on the same plane."

"Do you still have that globe?"

"Of course I do. I still go to it sometimes, turn it on and re-member that I was a daughter once. It's no ordinary globe. To me, it's magic."

"I can call up a globe on the Internet," Luke says.

"Will you show it to me sometime?"

"Sure!"

"It's good to look at the world from different perspectives, don't you think?"

"I guess. Hey, can I try a chip?"

"Go ahead."

"You seem like an Indian from the Old West." Luke crunches away with a wry smile. "With your moccasins and braid and all. And the way you talk sometimes."

"Thanks."

"You're welcome, I guess."

"Now it's you're turn, Luke."

"My turn?"

"To play Expression."

"I don't have anything to say," he says.

Bravery calls me. "Do you want to say something about Stu?"

"Nothing to say." He shrugs. "My mom said he lost control of the car."

He lost control of the car, she claimed to Luke, to me, to every sympathetic ear. Amazing how she emerged, every hair in place. Ravishing, in shock, no doubt. Drama was always her style.

.   .   .

C L E O   C O M E S home in an upbeat mood toting Chinese carry-out in emerald-green bags. The gold-embossed name reads San Francisco Dynasty.

"I don't eat Chinese," I say.

"Not so fast," she says. "There's Magnificent Moo Shu Vegetables and Beautiful Braised Tofu with Asparagus in here."

"They probably use oyster sauce or beef broth in all their dishes."

"God! Can't I do anything right?" she moans.

I hold my tongue.

"Marcy, I'm sorry I hung up so quickly. We were busy and I just wasn't sure where that conversation was going. Why were you trying to make me feel bad? Don't you think I feel bad enough?"

"Not bad enough to close down the plant and close your eyes and pay homage to your husband," I reply honestly.

"This *is* paying homage to Stu. He dreamed this for me, too. The timing is now. I've staked a good percentage of the last quarter's profits on this one show. I've banked on this one big moment. If I make it, I can buy the Bay. If I don't, I may have to leave it."

W I T H ,   O R without the children? Of course, my suspicions change the whole picture.

Go, Cleo, go. And don't ever come back.

.   .   .

CLEO SETS out a scandalous amount of food on the table. A banquet for two! I bring my bowl to the table.

"That same old soup?" Cleo nearly cries. "How can you eat the same thing night after night?"

"She threw in some lentils," Luke says.

"Yummy," Cleo jokes, handing her son a spring roll with delicate brass tongs. "So how was your day?"

"Some lady thought Marcy was you in Bayside Gourmet."

"That's a howl!" Cleo reacts. "You should have gone along with it, Marcy, and autographed a bottle for her!"

"Then we went out for lunch," Luke continues.

"Oh?" she says, impressed. "Where did you go?"

"The Umbrella Cafe."

"They buy my sauces by the truckload! They do the best calamari pasta on the Bay. Simple and succulent. What did you get, Luke?"

"The pizza."

"Like always," Cleo sings.

"I tried some of Marcy's whole-wheat chips. They tasted like tree bark," Luke says, teasing me.

"They were good, Luke," I protest.

He cracks up. "Yeah, for tree bark."

Cleo is all eyes.

HOMELESS PEOPLE are a stone's throw away but the trashcan is closer. With verve, she tosses out enough Chinese food to feed a shelter.

How could we be sisters?

. . .

JUST AS I'm nodding off, Cleo slips into my room. Sleep comes slowly here, in a bed now worn down with ancient dreams. Cleo's voice in the dark moves me. We have been here before.

"I knew you could snap him out of it," she says giddily. "What's your secret? What do you two talk about?"

"Dad."

10

WHY I worried so about my father was as deep and mysterious as the sea; I was certain other girls my age didn't. Meg didn't. Her father was so removed from her thoughts he may as well have been on Mars—at least in 1976. Before the decade was up she would guide him back to life after the death of her uncle Frank, his younger brother. I recall her saying his torment ended her youth. But for now, he was on Mars. Not that she didn't cherish him the way daughters do, but she didn't worry about him and fear for him and wonder about him the way I did for my father. He didn't live in her dreams and nightmares; she never woke up on a sweat-soaked pillow. Sometimes the fear stalked me and buried me alive; and if I closed my eyes too long, he would be gone forever.

One time Cleo told me something about my father that made me feel guilty for every Frito and Life Saver I had mindlessly eaten. It made me wish with all my powerless heart that I could have been reborn as his mother. I'd hug him and comfort him and praise him for every little thing. I'd skip my meals and spoon warm rice into his tummy. I'd let him loose in a field of flowers and let him play to exhaustion.

Growing up, my father had had few treats. Love was absent, as was supper most of the time. But one day his grandmother, whom he loved dearly, brought him a box of Sunmaid raisins. He stared and stared at the box, believing that the sun maid was Jesus Christ. He was mesmerized. His face flooded with hope, just gazing at his Sunmaid Jesus and eating his raisins, those sweet gems, one by one. In this way, in the midst of squalor, he drew his flame, his faith. And he believed his grandmother was the messenger of his faith. When she died not long after, he wept to himself in an emptied church, clutching his empty Sunmaid box like a Bible and wiping his tears on the rice-paper screen, one by one.

I w a s still on Wandering Lane, about to cross the street and cut through the woods to Tim and Tom's, when the tinny sounds of the Starland Vocal Band rode up behind me. Frog! An orange plastic transistor radio dangled from the handlebar of his mud-splattered moped.

"Hey, buttercup," he purred, "how about a little afternoon delight?"

I could've run across the street, disappeared into the woods, and lost him. But I didn't. Now he paced me very, very closely. His hot nostrils flared my way.

"Why be shy when you can be sexy, buttercup?"

"Quit calling me buttercup," I stammered.

"Look at what you're wearing," Frog shrugged. "Sure makes sense to me."

I remembered what I had on—the smock top with the buttercup print, courtesy of Cleo. No number of dress rehearsals in the mirror could make me cool today.

"How about showing me what's blooming underneath there?" he said, pretending to peek.

Mortified, I took off to the sound of his famous last words: "Miss Moonface loves me!"

TO WALK *the Sky Path* stirred something in Tim and Tom. We would sit in the kitchen and they would read aloud in perfect rhythm like frogs croaking in the dark, experiencing the midnight canoe ride of the characters Billie and Mush Jim.

Afro was a rapt pupil, too. He would sit on the bay windowsill while Mrs. Duncan drank coffee in the living room.

After each chapter, Tim and Tom and I would hold a short discussion.

"The teacher should be expelled from school," Tim said. "She makes Charlie feel bad about being an Indian."

"Like it's against the law to be different," Tom said.

"It was his Indian duty to go frogging on the creek."

"I'd rather go frogging than do my stupid homework."

The boys high-fived each other with a harmonious "Cactus Bear!," unaware that their father had come home and was standing in the doorway. Major Duncan was well over six feet tall with a shock of hair so blond it was almost white. Always in uniform, always fuming.

"I don't like the sound of what I'm hearing," he said. "Marcy, I pay you to straighten out their crossed eyes when they read so they won't be kicked back to kindergarten. I don't pay you to teach them this Indian crap."

"But it's a really good book," I replied.

Tim and Tom wanted to stand up for me, for the book, but their voices were mere squeaks.

"I don't care if it's a good book. It's about damn Indians. Now why don't you take the book home and bring another one over tomorrow?"

Afro went wild, barking up a storm from the windowsill.

"Get that nigger mutt out of my sight!" Major Duncan yelled.

Afro scurried out of the kitchen and up the stairs, out of sight. He was probably shaking like a leaf under a bed. Mrs. Duncan yelled back from the living room, "Oh, go pick on someone your own size!"

He'd handle her later, but for now Major Duncan had me to command. "What's your phone number? I'll call you later from the office with a list of more appropriate books."

I told him my phone number and watched him scribble it down on a napkin. The problem was, he inverted the last four numbers.

"No, it's 5564," I pointed out.

He gave me a glare that could wipe out a whole village of little dark people. I was the enemy now, I had crossed the line, witnessed something I wasn't supposed to see.

I took the book home and never brought it back.

. . .

THE WORLD was a terrible place, I decided, for creatures like Tim and Tom and Billie and Mush Jim and Afro and me. We were not safe, people were out there to hurt us. As I turned up Wandering Lane, I vowed to block Frog Fitzgerald out of my wandering mind. He could cross my bodily path but not my spiritual one. From now on, he was a whiff of skunk. I was my father's girl from now on.

WHEN I got home Cleo was cramping up over a pan of sizzling French toast.

"Someone's sticking me with pins," she breathed as though blood were seeping from the corners of her mouth. "There's so much goddamn evil out there. Shit, it's everywhere. People want to poke my eyes out for just breathing the same fucking air as them."

My mother was hysterical, reliving the outbreak of war with a spatula in her hand. "Marcy, get Owen. He in backyard. Take us to Dr. Choi. Hurry up!"

OWEN SPED to County Hospital with Cleo groaning and flopping about semiconsciously in the front seat, cursing every bump in the road.

"Shit! Fuck! Damn it all to hell!"

"Why not we go to Dr. Choi?" my mother kept asking.

"Who?" Owen asked.

"He Cleo doctor. She go to him when she sick last week," my mother explained.

"This is an emergency, Mom," I butted in.

Owen agreed. "Mama Moon, your daughter needs more than a thermometer."

Cleo gagged on her own obscenities, spitting them out at the speed of light.

"Marcy," Owen wondered, "what exactly was wrong with Cleo last week?"

I shrank. "I don't remember."

"You don't?"

"She have flu," my mother said.

"Right," I said, "the flu."

"Doesn't look like any flu I've ever seen," Owen remarked.

"Shut up, everyone," Cleo cried. "I had an abortion!"

"What?" Owen said.

"What?" my mother asked.

Cleo squinted at them with a look that would frighten God.

"An abortion. I had a goddamn botched abortion. Now, everyone shut the fuck up!"

Without a word, Owen floored it.

After a mile-long silence, my mother spoke up.

"What 'abortion' mean?"

THE EMERGENCY room was a bad dream, packed with tired faces. The staff was inattentive as Cleo lay helplessly on a cot, screaming her eyeballs out. How many times did they walk by her without a blink? No doctors, no nurses available yet. Five excruciating hours later, she was finally examined.

Afterward I went in to see her—she was calling for me. She looked strange, drained of life. Her lipstick and blush had smeared off but her painted-on eyes looked huge and hollow.

"The jackass pried open both holes and split me up the seams. After that, death will be a visit to the spa."

"Don't say that, Cleo. You're going to be okay, aren't you?"

"Unfortunately, yeah."

"How did you get sick in the first place? I mean, what exactly is wrong with you?"

"I got an infection from the abortion. One of those Petunia nurses probably wiped her fat ass with a glove and stuck it up me," she said, deadpan. "I could have died, *merci beaucoup*."

"Thank Owen," I said, just in case she forgot.

"Right," she remembered, and then it all came back to her in big, horrific waves. "I told Mom, didn't I?"

I nodded regretfully.

Somehow Cleo mustered up all her might; she took my shoulders and shook me from the bottom of her scared soul.

"Don't you dare tell Dad about this. When you write him, tell him all's well from this edge of the earth. You breathe one word and I'm history."

FOR HER to believe that, she didn't know the same parent I did. My father wasn't blind, he knew all about Cleo, and he still loved her and would always love her. It was not easy for him to endure the hurt, but it was better than losing a daughter, better than being unloved. We were all he had, besides my mother. That he rarely interfered was a reflection of how fragile he believed our bonds were.

WHEN I got home I reached into the mailbox, quite confident of what I would pull out. Indeed, among the mail was a big postcard for me. This one depicted an outdoor market crowded with dark-skinned women wearing loose-fitting garments. On their heads were turbans and on the turbans were straw baskets brimming with produce. The postcard's description read: *Village market scene (Bali).*

My darling Marcy,
I am writing this at the Bali airport waiting for the plane to Jakarta. The plane is delayed as usual, so I was rushing around this morning for nothing! No, that is not true. It allows me some time to jot down nice thoughts to my younger daughter, whom I miss very much. Two weeks seems like two years apart from the family. How can I last six more weeks? Perhaps being bogged down in work is a blessing in disguise.

This morning I watched a Bali dance, then took a look around the countryside. I bought a wood carving and a painting. You must help me decide what goes where in the house.

I trust you are all fine and taking your vitamins every day. Will write from Jakarta.

Love, Dad

*P.S. Did I mention my flight into Nepal? I arrived in Kat-
mandu under the foothills of the Himalaya Mountains. I
could see the tallest mountain peaks in the world from the
plane as we approached the airport. It was, as you young
people say, out of sight!*

Cleo was hospitalized for a few days. My mother was oddly
stoic through it all. She brought Cleo a deck of cards, a stack of
blue airmail letters, and her fall semester schedule of classes,
never mentioning the A word. We accompanied Owen whenever he went to visit her, which was usually twice a day, between shifts at Bean Cleaners and a night class he was taking.
In her drugged state, was Cleo warming up to him?

On the day of her scheduled release, Owen brought her a
stuffed panda with a red heart sewn on its bosom. She gritted
her teeth and said, "You're a sweetheart."

The minute Owen and my mother stepped out to the cafeteria, Cleo updated me with stories about the Petunia nurses on
her floor.

"Nurse Pigfoot jabs me in the butt with a needle like it's my
fault God gave her a snout for a nose. Next time she pulls that,
I'm going to barbecue her hand and serve it up in the cafeteria.
Hog hand, anyone?"

In the midst of her Petunia-bashing I took note of a bouquet
of red and white carnations by her bed.

"Who are those from?"

"Nurse Yanofsky," she sang.

"Who?"

"You know, the nice nurse from the clinic. The only one who gave a shit whether I made it out of there alive. She's an angel, li'l one—like you, only closer to heaven. Though for the life of me I can't figure out how she knew I was here."

An abrupt knock on the door silenced her. In stepped the doctor who had performed her abortion. His white coat gave him away.

"I just wanted to check in on you and make sure you've been comfortable, dear," he said with utmost insincerity.

"I'm okay," she snapped.

"These things happen. Not very often, thank goodness, but they do."

Cleo nodded stonily.

"Young lady, you might recall a form you signed prior to your abortion," he continued.

"A form?"

"Yes. It was given to you after your counseling session. Ring a bell?"

"Vaguely."

"The form waives your right to make any claim against me following the abortion."

"What exactly are you saying?"

"My dear, you do speak English, don't you?"

She froze. "Yes."

"Good. Then listen very carefully: Don't even think about taking any legal action. It would be a waste of your time and money. Just get some rest, go home, and chalk it up to lousy luck."

Cleo clutched her panda, motionless. When he closed the door behind him, she crumbled. She didn't stand up for herself or dispose of him like a bag of trash. But all the way home she muttered in the back seat like she was in some sort of trance, "He deserves to die, he deserves to die. . ."

C L E O   R E C O V E R E D and went back to work at Songs & Bongs. She worked overtime, from ten to ten, to make up for lost hours. At least that's the story she gave us. Maybe she was just avoiding my mother—they had not discussed what had happened. That would be as painful as the infection itself.

M A J O R   D U N C A N never did call me with a list of books. So I came up with a new strategy: the game of Omok. I dusted off my Paduk board from the basement and brought it over for our next session. My theory? Rearrange their brain cells and put them back in their right order. Of course, Tim and Tom fought over seniority—that is, who got to use the honorable white stones.

"I'm older! I was born twelve minutes before you!" Tim insisted.

"So why do you act like such a dumb juvenile?" Tom shot back.

As it turned out, diplomacy was the answer. They would alternate using the white stones.

Omok proved to be a cathartic experience for Tim and Tom. They didn't fight or lose their cool. The mere act of moving a stone held the weight of a world decision. Whoever won said, "Cactus Bear."

One morning Mrs. Duncan called me away from the game and into the living room, where she sat on the couch, as always.

"Yes, Mrs. Duncan?"

She patted the cushion next to her. Her coffee splashed without a care.

"Why do the boys say 'Cactus Bear'?" she wondered drowsily. "I've asked them but they won't give me a straight answer. What's a Cactus Bear?"

"It was a papier-mâché bear we made in school," I said.

"A papier-mâché bear?"

"We got an A-plus on it and it became their symbol of success."

"Symbol of success?"

"Yes, and now when they say it, it means they're doing all right," I explained.

She sighed with sleepy contemplation. "Now, this game they're playing, it's going to help them at school?"

"I hope so. It might help them concentrate better."

She drooled, then murmured, "Um."

"Are you okay, Mrs. Duncan? Mrs. Duncan?"

Her eyes, then head, rolled back; her body went limp. I took her cup from her and smelled something in her coffee that wasn't creamer. It was something I had smelled on Cleo's breath after a night of hard-core partying.

Oh, our secret lives…

11

THE DARKNESS in Cleo was conceived long ago. It found a spot in her heart and burrowed itself deep. There were signs a naïve girl like me couldn't see. Her calling Tim and Tom upside-down monkeys, and the waitress in Subs, Etc. a hoagie hog—and that was when Cleo was in a good mood.

Now I can see it in black and white, without the rosy vision of a little sister in love. And what I see is this: Only a ghost of the young woman who could calm my father in his emotional storms remains, and this ghost is off elsewhere, a shadow moving in my memories. What's left behind can be labeled as Cleo's Creations.

The Global Gourmet Food Show is all that sizzles her, like sauce on a hot wok. So Luke is on the back burner, so June Moon is stuck in some odd nook. So what? Once Cleo ran away from her family, ran far from home, never to return. Now she's about to do it again.

Even if she does return, are her children really safe in her clutches?

I SHUDDER when I think about what happened the morning after Cleo brought home that fancy Chinese food. She went to bed giddy but woke up bitchy; tripped over something, cursed, and threw her hairbrush down the stairs. That Luke was gone and I was feeding June Moon a bottle of soy milk only incensed her more. She spotted the soy milk carton on the counter and squinted.

"What's this you're feeding my daughter?"

"Organic soy milk."

"And what's wrong with the real thing?"

"*Every*thing. Besides, June Moon loves soy milk. Look at her drinking it, like it's saving her life. And Luke poured some on his cereal this morning."

"My daughter doesn't need her life saved," Cleo announced, snatching June Moon's bottle out of her puckering lips. "And she doesn't need that soy shit either."

June Moon's sleepy eyes opened with shock. Then the screaming began. I held her tiny frightened body to my chest while Cleo flew into a rage. The bottle landed in the trash, followed by the carton.

"Stop crying, do you hear me? Just shut up for one minute! Sometimes I get so sick of this! Oh, so both my children drink soy milk? Sure, everyone drinks soy shit but me!"

.   .   .

FRIDAY, THE morning of Cleo's departure. Her bags are at the door, but her heart is halfway to New York. She cradles June Moon good-bye for five seconds, then hands her back to me.

"Sell boatloads of sauce," I say.

"Come on, Marcy, don't belittle my moment. You have your Moccathon and I have the Global Gourmet Food Show. Let's at least respect each other's big moments during our time together."

Our time together? She's in and out, never here in spirit. I speak from experience: Once she leaves, she's gone. *I love my children,* she said, but she's two steps from desertion.

"You're right. Good luck, Cleo."

"Thanks," she says. "Look, I guess I won't see you until Wednesday afternoon and Thursday is your Moccathon, so this is almost it, I guess. Will you be leaving Wednesday afternoon or night?"

"I haven't decided."

"Well, I'll call around dinnertime every day, okay?"

"Yes."

"And you have my number at the Plaza."

"Yes."

"And at the show, Booth 1127."

"Yes."

"And call, for heaven's sakes. How on earth did you develop phone phobia?"

"Yes."

She gives up, goes for the door. But something stops her short. "I'm glad Luke's coming to his senses. But it would have been nice if he'd hung around long enough to see me off this morning. It's seven-thirty; my God, what time does he get up? Does the boy ever sleep?"

The boy sleeps but doesn't dream. How could anyone dream under this palatial roof? When it rains, no one hears it. The moon above is so far removed. True, Luke has opened up, but most of the time only a barely visible crack. His aura gives off dying light. If he suspects what I suspect about Cleo, I've got to get him away from here before it's snuffed out forever.

BECAUSE IT all boils down to this: Cleo cannot always have her way. The world is not hers to step on. If my father had given her a globe that could light up, maybe the world would have looked and felt different to her. Maybe her mind would have spun in another direction. Maybe her darkness would have never materialized.

12

THERE WAS a time I would have given up my whole collection of *American Teen* magazines to have a boy love me the way Owen loved Cleo. Owen symbolized all boys, what I sought out in the sky on those eternal summer nights when Cleo was out and my mother was playing Solitaire and my father was halfway around the globe. I longed to be in a boy's—any boy's—arms. I longed to be what *American Teen* magazine called "The Wonder Girl in the Universe."

And yet I was not Cleopatra Moon.

I did not possess her magic, the spell she cast over even the groggiest stranger. I did not possess her myth, what she dreamed up in the minds of all men cruising the aisles of Drug Fair. I did not possess her figurine body or hair that moved like the ocean when she walked her goddess walk. I did not drive fairer girls to gossip.

And then I heard it louder than my dad's plane taking off: *Miss Moonface loves me.*

M E G   A N D I used to ask her eight ball if we would ever meet the boys of our dreams. We would keep asking until the answer we wanted came up. We also tried to call back famous dead guys like the Kennedy brothers and Martin Luther King, Jr., on her Ouija board. None bothered to tremble any message our way. The eight ball was harmless fun, but the Ouija board summoned fear in my father.

"Girls, please do not engage in that foolish activity under my roof," he'd say. "Play Monopoly instead."

When he caught Meg and me holding a séance in the basement, all hell broke loose. Meg was trying to contact her grandmother, who had passed away in her sleep, to make sure she was warm enough, because she was always cold without her quilt. My father heard us chanting, "Grandma Campbell, wake up from your nap." He thumped down the stairs and blew out our candle.

"You are both smart girls. Why must you find it necessary to engage in such foolish activity?"

"I just wanted to see how my grandma was doing. Please don't be mad, Mr. Moon," Meg implored him.

"Don't be mad, Dad," I pleaded.

"Meg, your grandmother, she was a dressmaker during the Depression, was she not? And she took care of a whole family without a husband, is this right?"

"Yes, sir," Meg said.

"Yah! She took care of herself then and I believe she is taking care of herself now. Don't disturb her, it is not your place. Spirits belong in the afterlife, not in my basement. Once you bring them back, they might get lost. I am quite fond of you, Meg, but if you insist on this foolish activity, you cannot spend the night with Marcy anymore. I am sorry."

The next morning, after Meg packed her things and went home, my father came to my bedroom. He had that stern, lecture look about him. Instead, he told me he had witnessed an exorcism in a small village when he was a teenager. That's all he would say. To this day, it haunted him.

"Don't fool around with the supernatural, Marcy. You might wake up the devil instead."

THESE DAYS my mother had quieted down to a hush. Her pot-and-pan clatter was merely a memory. Mostly she just cooked in between games of Solitaire. I leaned over the pan while she grilled sesame-marinated beef for us. Cleo was working late.

With her oversized ivory chopsticks, she turned the strips of beef. "I want to go home," she bitterly announced.

A fragrant smoke went up like dreams.

"But you are home," I said. "You hardly ever leave the house."

"No, *my* home. My hometown."

"In North Korea?"

She nodded.

"Sunchun?" I said.

Just hearing the name of her hometown moved her; her face sagged in the bleak light through the kitchen window.

"Waterfall splashing all over place. Fruit so sweet and juicy I can still taste. Harvest time big, big celebration. Everyone, all ages, have good time. Winter we ice skate across river, race, race, race, then eat hot chestnut. Mostly, I win."

"But you can't go back there, Mom. No one can go there. Not even President Ford."

"I spend whole childhood in country cut off from rest of world. Why *my* country? All my friends, gone. All my family, gone with the wind. Why I am here? Can't speak normal. Can't drive to A&P like other mother. Husband, ocean away. Daughter, both stranger. What my purpose to live for?"

"Mom, you have everything to live for. Who would cook and clean for us?"

"I don't want to cook and clean for you!" she spat out. "You not family I love!"

I didn't say a word.

"Marcy"—she was choking with apology—"I can't express like American mom."

"That's okay," I said.

My mother slumped into an old woman; her ivory chopsticks slipped through her fingers and onto the floor like fallen dreams. "I wish I could be mom you love."

By the grace of God and a long humbling prayer, her spirit lifted during supper. It was the clear soup in a black lacquer bowl, the wilted scallions weaving through the plate of beef,

and a neat row of small dishes brimming with cold spicy vegetables that always brightened her up. My mother was blessed
with a hearty appetite and this evening the little girl in
Sunchun eating furiously with her chopsticks came to life.

"Marcy, eat more rice!"

With a large wooden spoon, she heaped a sticky white
mound on my plate and another on hers.

"More *bulgogi*, too! Don't want to get so thin like Cleo. Weak
girl! No meat on bones, that why she always get so sick. If wind
blow, Cleo fall down, can't get up. Good, delicious food make
you strong. Look at Owen, he eat like horse."

"A lovesick horse," I said.

"What lovesick horse mean?"

"It means Owen's in love with Cleo."

"Poor Owen, he dreamer like father. Father mortgage house
to keep dry-cleaning business. He say he run competition out of
town. Just a dream." She shrugged regretfully. "My dream to go
back and change history. But that a song, impossible dream.
Dumb dream! No, I dream you grow up like Madame Curie.
And Cleo straighten out head, marry decent man. And Daddy
blood pressure go down and parents drop dead."

"Mom!"

She hid her mischievous smile by cupping her bowl of soup
and taking a drink. "Marcy, you make me promise, okay?"

"Sure, Mom."

"You don't act like Cleo and walk around like *kisaeng* girl, do
it for money. You are virgin when you marry."

"Okay," I said.

. . .

D E S P I T E   M Y promise, sin dangled itself before me like a pair of Cleo's prized earrings and I couldn't resist—I snatched at its temptation. Meaning I found myself back in Cleo's room that night, trying on all the clothes I had missed in recent days. Her gold mini-dress with the negligee sleeves, her black netted tank top. Beaded things, satin things, lacy things. I was buttoning up a jewel-studded denim vest when Cleo's icy reflection appeared in the mirror.

"Just what do you think you're doing?"

"Nothing," I lamely replied.

The heap of clothes on her bed was a mountain of evidence against me.

"You call going through my stuff *nothing*?"

"No."

"I'm in shock!" she wailed, then she zeroed in on me, her li'l demon sister. "Who do you think you are? It was bad enough in the dorm with all those Petunia piglets stealing my stuff off the drying rack. All they left me was my underwear and only because their fumes would split the crotch. These are my things, not yours! When I was your age I wore kilts and saddle shoes!"

"I wasn't going to wear them anywhere."

She shoved me against her closet with one arm and undid buttons with the other.

"Damn right you're not!"

C L E O   H A D a cruel, biting, poisonous streak, but like the liquor on her breath it always wore off. A short while later she stood over my bed in her pink robe and slippers, shuffling sorrowfully. There I was, a mangy mutt, rereading my "Dream On" essay, wishing I were dead.

"Sorry I yelled at you, li'l one. What do you expect working twelve hours a day with only two cigarette breaks? I live on coffee and Tab, you know. All the caffeine and Saccharin sends me into overdrive."

"It's not your fault. I shouldn't have been in your closet in the first place."

"I'm a skunk. Spit on me."

"No, Cleo!"

She hopped on my bed and my essay went flying. "Knock my teeth out!"

"Cleo!" I squealed.

"Break my bitchy bones," she cried, tickling me into euphoria. "Kick me in the butt! Ring my neck! Poke my eyes out with chopsticks and drop 'em in soup!"

Later, in a huffing, puffing, teary-eyed sweat: "I know you want to grow up, Marcy. It's as natural as taking a dump a day. But being an adult isn't all it's cracked up to be. Look at Mom— what she'd do to be a girl again, sharing pink and green *mochis* with her brothers. And Dad. God! With age came pills, stress, insomnia, dreams, nightmarish revelations. You're only young once is a cliché, but it's true."

"But you like being grown up, don't you, Cleo? You can do what you want. Dress up and be someone special."

"You're only special if you're special in here," she said, touching my heart. "And you are special. You've been special since the minute you were born and christened my li'l sister. Catch my drift?"

"Caught."

"By the way, when did those boobs happen?"

LATER, AS I lay in bed, her fingerprints and kneeprints still all over me, her spirit still in the room, I realized how much I needed that tickle, the warmth of my big sister, which might not always be there. I feared it would be all over too quickly, already a memory if I closed my eyes. It would vanish in my dreams. She would be gone. Only her angry echo would remain.

While I was sleeping, Cleo must have sneaked into my room. When I woke up her denim vest was hanging in my closet like the Hope diamond. I slipped it on, knowing it was mine. I looked in the mirror. I was razzle-dazzled.

I WORE that vest over a T-shirt every day for the rest of the summer. It looked like it had survived being washed up on a thousand shores. Like it had lived through a thousand dusty, hitchhiking summers. Blue, green, and red glass jewels glittered with decadence. The beat-up faded look defined its beauty; it put a lifetime of name-calling on a road behind me.

MY NEW look prompted me to do two things. First, I stopped sending half my tutoring money to Peace of Mind Charity. Second, I bought myself a tube of Berry Cherry lip gloss from Drug Fair, and a pair of high wedgy sandals from

Satisfaction—with Cleo's half-hearted nod. Not that I had any-where to wear my sandals, but the mere existence of them in my closet catapulted me to Cleo status.

I could no longer afford to give away my money when I had me, in the mirror, to think about.

IT HAPPENED on a Saturday morning. Tim and Tom had begged me to preside over their Omok championship game. That their father would be home had slipped my mind.

"What's going on here?"

"We're playing Omok," I replied.

"What the hell—?"

"It's a game. You try to get five stones in a row while blocking your opponent at the same time."

"Never heard of it."

"It's a Korean game."

"I see," he said.

"It's fun, Dad," Tim said.

"We're tied dead even. Ten to ten," Tom added.

"And just how is this Korean game going to help my sissy sons read like everyone else?" Major Duncan asked me.

"Leave them alone and let them play!" his wife shouted.

He'd punch her lights out later, but he ignored her for now. "I asked you a question, Marcy."

I couldn't think.

"Are you deaf?"

I mumbled idiotic things.

"Speak up!"

"Marcy," Tim butted in, "you play him."

Major Duncan looked at his son, stunned.

"Play him, Marcy," Tom nodded.

Oh, how Major Duncan wanted to smack them silly, smack them to the ground where they belonged, at his feet, in his domain.

"No," I said.

But I was not boss. I was in his house, under his rule. Major Duncan pulled up a chair and said with a cruel tick, "Let's play."

I was in no position to disobey him, even though I had not actually played Omok in several years. My mother had given it up, Cleo was no good, and my father loved the thought of me being champ too much to challenge me.

I went over the rules of Omok with Major Duncan and we began.

LIBERATION WAS an unlawful concept in the Duncan household. But if I witnessed the word defined, it was on the faces of Tim and Tom as I beat their father, hands down, six quick games in a row. I knew they were silently cheering for me. What did it matter that Major Duncan was an inexperienced player? He was older and in charge, now defeated and humiliated. He grabbed Afro by his curly neck.

"You damn nigger mutt!" he hollered.

"Stop it!" we all shouted.

Afro went flying across the kitchen, followed by the bowl of white stones and Major Duncan's last words to me: "You're fired! Don't come back to this house! Ever!"

.   .   .

WALKING HOME, I felt sick to my stomach. Not for me.
I had won, I was the champ. And I had made Major Duncan
look like a fool in front of the sons he ridiculed with such per-
verse pleasure. But I felt sick for Tim and Tom, who needed
not me but someone of Herculean might to save them from
that house of hell. I had planned to make a papier-mâché bear
as a trophy for the winner of the tournament, but now I knew
this would never materialize. Their fate seemed linked to the
real Cactus Bear. Lost, stolen, gone.

Something else sticks out in my mind: How I wanted to steal
Afro from Major Duncan's evil clutches. The poor, helpless
thing. For days I thought about how I could sneak into their
house and sneak Afro out. *Come here, Afro, come here.* I always
regretted the world I left him in, battered and shivering.

13

L I K E A peasant running from bombs, I try to gather the children, hustle them toward the door. Luke isn't budging.

"Where are we going?"

"To the bus station!"

"Why?"

"This is your chance to see wide open sky with your soul on fire from the sun, Luke!"

"See what?"

"I'm taking you and June Moon to my home for a few days. It'll be an adventure you won't find anywhere, not even on the Internet. You'll smell the desert instead of the Bay and watch the moon rise over cacti. Mountains will rise in your eyes and change your vision forever. We'll go on the Moccathon and shake out our kinks. We'll have a great time."

"Does my mom know about this?"

"No, but why should you stay here another day when I'm telling you there's a place called White Sky that will make the loner in you crave all-day solitude?"

L U K E   B O A R D S the bus as if he has nothing better to do anyway. His passivity will fade as soon as we roll into the Nevada sunset.

June Moon is fussy. I feed her, tell her all about the primitive sounds of White Sky—the winds, the spirits, the stampeding ghosts of wild horses—and how she will fall into a lovely, guided sleep the moment I set her down.

"Have you ever been on a long bus trip before?" I ask Luke.

He nods with fond, fading memory. "My mom and I used to go everywhere by Greyhound. Once the bus broke down in the middle of nowhere and we hitchhiked to a campground. We met some bikers. They cooked us chili from a can and let us sleep in their tent. It was smoky in there."

Those were Cleo's gypsy days, before she met Stu. Home was wherever she hung out. She was a free woman, ask any renegade on the road.

"Luke, now that San Francisco is behind you, is there something you want to say? Anything?"

The road leads Luke into a state of silence.

"Luke, I'm here for you. I'm all yours."

He shifts uncomfortably out of his silence. "When can I call my mom?"

.   .   .

UPSTAIRS, PABLO and I have no phone; the thought of it makes us jump. Downstairs in Cactus Bear, there is one that rings under the rubble. Too many calls and it's off the hook.

Chimes are a different animal; their sound is magical, mystical, not urgent. We love their sound, we invite them into our home at any hour.

THE BUS to White Sky is actually a bus to Mesa Crossing, the neighboring town. Buses don't make it out to White Sky and the spirits thank us.

We walk to White Sky on foot. The path is deserted, though well worn with moccasins. June Moon is strapped to my back, Luke is kicking his imaginary stone. A late-summer afternoon falls over us. The air is still and hot and pungent with sage.

San Francisco drifts toward the back of my mind, recedes into the fog.

In spirit, I have not left White Sky for one minute. Not only is the terrain of the Great Basin etched in me but also the air that speaks to me with every step. Laid out like beautiful earthenware are rabbitbrush and rocks and flowering cacti. I am almost home.

Coming upon Cactus Bear, I know that I, the once dreamy-eyed li'l sister, will be the heroine of this story. It is all clear to me like a vision through rain. Not only am I going to single-handedly out-walk everyone and raise the money to build an herbal healing clinic, not only will the White Sky magic return, but I'm saving two more helpless souls. Not from disease or poverty but something just as deadly. The hands of Cleo. Her darkness. Her loveless heart. Otherwise, June Moon would grow up with blank eyes. Luke would grow hunchbacked with despair.

I had no choice.

P A B L O ' S   O N the front porch swing, minding Cactus Bear. He spots something—us. His good eye squints with disbelief. At some point his bones become sand. We are not a mirage. He leaps up to greet me, hugs me with the heart of a lonely hermit.

"What's this?" he whispers.

"Pablo, meet June Moon and Luke."

"Cleo's kids?"

"Yeah," Luke confirms.

Pablo pauses to admire both children. "No one told me we were having guests, but our home is your home."

"You live in the store?" Luke asks.

"Our living quarters are upstairs," Pablo explains, escorting him in.

"Where the higher spirits live," I add.

The floors creak, welcoming me home.

P A B L O   M I S S E D a nervous breakdown by a hair and some-times his edges give him away. Sometimes his steady, bohemian voice is too controlled. Sometimes his rumpled presence begs for one of the suits he left hanging in his L.A. apartment. Some-times his brilliance is dulled by long Nevada afternoons, as he watches tumbleweeds pass him by. Someday—if he stays—when his face is weathered from fifty years of desert living, this will be the only life he chooses to remember.

"I missed you," he says.

"I missed you, too."

We're in our bedroom, cleaning cobwebs from corners. How I've missed this place. Our bare floors, a bed worn down with dreams. Just downstairs, Cactus Bear, the shop that never quite closes. No matter what hour, we welcome the sound of chimes. June Moon is still strapped to me, her cheek warms my back. Luke is checking out the shop.

"You could have called," Pablo says.

"You could have called me," I say.

"You're the one who walked out angry. If I called you first, it would be like I was begging for your forgiveness. The first sign of subordination and it's over. I've seen client after client get screwed by an auditor just for twitching."

"Let it go," I warn him.

He sighs, lets it go.

"Pablo, I forgive you for saying I had an immature attitude toward Cleo, because I never told you the whole story. Right or wrong, I did go to San Francisco with a chip on my shoulder. But guess what I returned with?"

"Her baby on your back?"

"Yes, and you know why?"

"No. Why?"

"Because I'm saving her from a life with Cleo. We can give Luke and June Moon all the love and spiritual nourishment in the world they need."

"What's wrong with a life with Cleo? She *is* their mother."

"Biologically, yes. But they're like hairs in her comb, not missed."

"How can you say such a thing?"

"Cleo thinks nothing of up and leaving them just days after Stu's supposed accident. Yes, I'm serious, she's at a trade show, all in the name of making more money."

"Stu's *supposed* accident?"

"She's dangerous, I'm telling you. Her temper rules her. There's something suspicious about the, quote, *accident*. I think Cleo had a hand in steering the car off the road, just to get back at him for having a modern-day Petunia. Another woman, I mean."

I have never witnessed horror cross Pablo's face and it is a spectacularly odd sight. His good eye bulges out at me, the other floats in outer space.

I stand my ground. "So I took her children. I had no choice. I have to protect them."

Pablo backs away from me. He doesn't get it. For a new account, Cleo would caress his neck and slit his throat in the same stroke.

"Don't look at me like *I'm* the criminal," I say. "They're under my wing. I have a sense of responsibility here. I know what it's like to be left all alone in the world with no one to turn to."

He feebly feels his way to the bed.

"Marcy, what have you done? Do you know how much trouble you could get into? You're a kidnapper. A fugitive! I had clients thrown in jail for lesser crimes!"

"Let it go, Pablo."

He sighs, lets it go again.

I loosen June Moon from me and hold her up against a wall hanging of birds and bears for Pablo to behold.

"Look at her. Look at her, Pablo."

Pablo utters, "She's beautiful. I smell spit and baby powder."

"She's the baby you've always wanted."

"But she's not a White Sky baby," he says.

There's something biblical about the way June Moon wiggles as I lower her into Pablo's arms.

"June Moon is every baby in the universe," I breathe.

As Pablo takes her from me, I know I am not getting her back. Her very touch heals him.

14

I COULD not tell my mother that Major Duncan had fired me. Surely she would call me a worthless daughter. So after summer school I would loiter around the neighborhood, walk to the 7-Eleven and buy powdered candy. One such morning, two steps from my front door, something even more monumental than being fired would happen to me. It was a rumbling in the street that set it all in motion.

"Calling Miss Moonface!"

Cleo's vest empowered me for a moment I had played over in my head like a scratched record. I turned around. There he was on his moped, shaggier than ever. Frog Fitzgerald in a black Aerosmith T-shirt and the same frayed jeans.

"What do you want?" I shouted.

"Come here and I'll tell you!" he shouted back.

"Why should I?"

"Don't be afraid, Miss Moonface! You won't get a good buzz if you mix fear with fun!"

"I said, what do you want?"

"To talk, that's all! Any law against that?"

"Talk about what?"

He shrugged his bony shoulders knowing he was trouble on wheels and proud of it.

"A four-letter word!" he shouted.

"What four-letter word?"

"Love!" he declared.

Whatever compelled me to take that long, slow, treacherous walk down my lawn remains a mystery. Walking toward Frog my legs almost gave out I was so self-conscious of the sun on my just-washed hair and my swaying hips. My walk lasted forever until a million heartbeats later, when I finally reached the curb.

"Dig the jacket," he said.

"It's a vest."

"Far out." He grinned cheekily. "Why don't you take it off?"

"Why?"

"So I can see what's underneath."

"Why should I?"

"'Cause it's steaming hot out here. Hot enough to go skinny dipping at Rainbow Run. What do you say?"

"No way," I said.

Frog read the shock on my face and laughed horribly. Then he zipped down the street doing his Jimmy Durante: "I love Miss Moonface!"

.   .   .

N o t a wink did I sleep that night nor the night after that
nor the night after that. With every toss and turn and peek at
my clock radio whenever the grandfather clock downstairs
chimed, I heard *I love Miss Moonface*. If you don't meet yourself in the pitch dark, you never will, and I did. What I had secretly hoped for all along was true: Frog Fitzgerald loved me. I
took this revelation and squeezed it with my pillow, praying it
all meant what I thought it meant.

And then it seemed to me there was a change in our household. Cleo had never been quite the same since her infection.
She would inch toward the old Cleo, then back off as though
she had entered some latent stage of recovery and was taking
some old-fashioned medicine. Nowadays the cabin was history
and guys calling for *Cleopatra, man* were dwindling by the day.
She gave up drinking and smoking pot. No more partying. At
six-fifteen on the dot she was home from work and cooking up
Korean food with some kind of crazed salvation zeal. *Guk bap,
kalbi, bulgogi*—a delicious smoke invaded the house. She put
on a few healthy pounds and her face took on a glow that would
make an angel sing. The face of Cleo was changing. Not the
painted-on eyes or the mink hair, but more in her expression,
which lost its danger—or so it seemed. She was still the goddess of all get-out, but without the racy accessories—dangle
earrings, snake bracelets, strappy sandals—or attitude. I didn't
make too much of it; I was too distracted.

After all, Frog was calling me day and night.

My mother banged on my door. "Marcy! Same boy again with low-class voice. Tell him go away or I make you call police!"

"Hello," I said breathlessly into the phone.

"Hello, Miss Moonface," he panted.

My mother shot me a dirty look, then proceeded to scalp a giant white radish.

"I wish you wouldn't call me that," I whispered.

"But it's beautiful. Miss Moonface with the beautiful moon breasts and beautiful moon hips going round and round and making me dizzy."

"Don't talk that way!"

"When I'm around you, there's a full moon out and I'm a wolf howling for your love."

"Stop it!"

"No can do, Miss Moonface. All year long you made me suffer on the bus. All I wanted was to sit next to you. Blow in your ear. Feel your leg. But you always turned the other way."

"I thought you were making fun of me."

"Oh, man! I was just trying to get your attention. Ask the gang, they know how hot I was for you. You drove my nuts nuts."

"What?"

"I was hot for you."

"You were?"

"Would I lie?"

Of course he would! But if I said yes, he might hang up on me, on what was keeping me up nights. What I was living for.

· · ·

I T   W A S   not uncommon for me to come downstairs and find Cleo and Owen on the couch eating from the large square wooden plates my father had brought back from the Philippines.

"All right, who is he?" Owen grinned over a plate of spicy transparent noodles topped with a mound of bean sprouts. "A boy from school?"

I was too aware of my mother playing Solitaire in the kitchen to reply.

"You're a little young to have a boyfriend, aren't you?"

"He's not my boyfriend."

"Damn right he's not," Cleo said, pointing her chopsticks at me. "Put your hair in pigtails and act your age, Marcy. Help Mit and Mot figure out who's who."

"Mit and Mot?" Owen questioned her.

"Her dyslexic students. Twins. When they learn how to drive, they'll brake for green. Picture them at a four-way stop." She cracked up.

"Tim and Tom Duncan," I explained to Owen. "But Cleo calls them Mit and Mot."

For a split second Owen looked at Cleo with disappointment, but her aura arrested him and he settled into a nerdy smile. Cleo could do that with a bloody dagger in her hand.

But Cleo would have none of him—or anyone else—these days. She entertained no notions of romance. That door was shut, locked, bolted. Owen had practically saved her life, so she was indebted to be friendly, at least. Offer food. Except in letters to my father and cooking up a storm, Cleo slowly grew dead to the world, in my eyes. So it surprised me when Nurse Yanofsky called her to thank her for the card and the John Denver album she had sent her.

M EG   W A S T E D no time blasting me to bits. She was talking a mile a minute, paying for the long-distance call with her hard-earned babysitting money, she informed me.

"Why didn't you just send me your obituary, Marcy Moon?"

"It's good to hear your voice, too, Meg."

"Anyone but Frog Fitzgerald!" she wailed. "What's gotten into you since I left Glover?"

"Maybe I've grown up."

"Excuse me while I puke! Marcy, he's out to hurt you, you know. Don't forget what he called you. *Miss Moonface.*"

"Because my face glows like a full moon," I reminded her. "Isn't that what you said?"

"I lied."

"Meg, why are you being so negative? Being two thousand miles away in Texas has changed you. You even sound different."

"My brother's getting a divorce."

"No way! Bill?"

"It's turning the whole family upside down! My dad won't talk about it, and my mom won't stop. We thought Bill and Jill were made for each other. Remember the wedding? Remember what everyone was saying?"

I could still hear the echoes of drunk adults and their clinking glasses around the Champagne fountain. "A marriage made in heaven," I said.

"More like hell. They're ice-cold around each other. Neither one will crack a smile. And get this: Bill's got another girlfriend and Jill's got someone else, too."

"No way!"

"And if you think that's bad, the baby's not even Bill's!"

"Baby Billy?"

"And here I'd thought he had Bill's pug nose when it was somebody else's. What a gross-out thought! My mom says it's re*pug*nant, get it? The moral of the story is: What you see is only half the picture."

"Our song!" I cried. "Meg?"

"Yeah?"

"How much more time can you talk?"

"Two, three minutes, tops."

"Okay, then, let's do it."

We broke into chorus:

"What you see is only half the picture,
What you hear is only half the song.
When you live in a fog of mad confusion
What you think is right is always wrong."

"I'm glad you're coming home, Meg." I hugged the phone. "I'm so glad."

AFTER WE hung up, it was as though I went under water and thought it all through and came up in a dreamy state. In this state, I studied the newest arrival from my father. This postcard was of a wide ancient temple of gray stone, flocked by natives and described as *Borobudur Temple during its annual ceremony*. The stamp revealed that he was writing from *Republik Indonesia*.

My darling Marcy,
I arrived here just before noon and had a nice traditional lunch of skewered meat and Indonesian-style rice. I can't believe I ate the whole thing! People are very friendly and try their very best to please the visitors. I spent almost three hours at the beach today, soaking up every leisure minute I could get. Most of the time it is go, go, go.
I am so proud that you are helping the Duncan boys with a variety of techniques and do not make them feel foolish. More children would excel if encouraging words fell upon their ears. You would make a fine teacher someday, if you so choose. Teaching is a noble profession, unlike the job of stockbroker or advertising executive. True, the salary is nothing to write home about. But money is unimportant when your spirit is consumed with greed, which is becoming all too common.
There is a Korean restaurant just across from the hotel, but I have not had the occasion to visit it yet. Maybe tomorrow. Not that I would ever compare their food to Mommy's meals. She has spoiled me for life. Anyone else's jijim pancakes taste like cardboard!
                                                            Love, Dad

It was so blindingly sunny I wasn't sure it was Frog bopping toward me as I stood with my cart at the A&P, waiting for Cleo to drive up. And then it all happened so fast. He stumbled into me like it was an accident and stole a kiss. Not a real kiss, just a peck on the cheek.

He grinned. "Been thinking of me?"

"No," I replied. "Well, maybe just a little."

"Just a little? That's like saying I almost don't count."

"I didn't say that."

"You beautiful, bejeweled thing, you don't get it. I'm waiting for the day I've got you moaning in your sleep."

There I stood in my beloved vest, speechless, dumbstruck, and above all the most beautiful, bejeweled thing on earth.

Cleo zoomed up the pickup lane and jumped out with an angry slam.

"Dig the car," Frog said, leaning against it. "My brothers work on them all the time. Take them apart and put them back together with their eyes closed. They own Brothers Auto Body. Ever heard of them?"

"Don't lean on it," she warned him, lifting bags of groceries. "I mean it, I don't even want to see your shadow on my car. Got it? Marcy, want to give me a hand here?"

"I've got to go," I said.

Frog brushed my face and said, "Ciao, Miss Moonface."

T H E   T O P was down but Cleo hit the roof.

"What did that punk call you? Miss Moonface? What is that supposed to mean?"

I shrugged. "It's just a nickname."

"It sounds derogatory."

"Derogatory?"

"Yeah, like you're some Hong Kong caricature. Some moon-faced madam."

"It's just a nickname!"

"Like your real name isn't good enough?"

"Your boyfriends call you Cleopatra!"

"So this punk's your boyfriend now?"

"Not exactly."

"He kissed you. Deny it and you're dead meat."

"So what if he kissed me?"

Cleo spun off the main drag and into the parking lot of a bank.

"I've seen that runt around town. He practically ran me off the road with that stupid scooter. Stay the hell away from him. He doesn't give two shits for you or anybody else."

"You don't know him," I said.

"What's to know? He's a damn dropout. A redneck without a cause. A future flunky from Fuck U. He doesn't know the meaning of respect, I know the type. If you were hanging from a cliff, he'd crack open another beer!"

"I guess you know the type," I muttered.

"What? What did you say?"

Even as the words sputtered from my lips, I couldn't believe I was saying them. "I mean, I didn't see any of your boyfriends at the clinic. Or the hospital."

Cleo squeezed back on the main drag and sped home without a word.

. . .

EVERYTHING CHANGED after that. Cleo disowned me, in a sense. Not that she didn't make a plate for me at supper, but anything I said was brushed off like dirt. Little Feat would say she was *cold, cold, cold*. Cold but civil. If I asked her if she wanted more scallions in the soy sauce, she would grunt yes. If I got hit by a truck, she might go through the motions and bury me, but she wouldn't pray for my soul. In honor of my father's birthday, she prepared his favorite—fish soup and sweet potato tempura—but ate in silence and cut the cake without offering me seconds. I had hurt her, it's true, but for once I put myself first.

As Frog would say, any law against that?

During this time, which by now was August, the face I'd worn for so long—loving daughter, li'l sister, faithful reader of *American Teen* magazine—was changing, too. While I applied Berry Cherry lip gloss, that innocent girl faded away. A girl like that went through life being lonely and laughed at. One day she'd look in the mirror and see an old Oriental maid with a white bun. No, things were different now. The sky opened up solely so the sun could beam down on me. The moon rose merely to shine through my window. I woke up and fell asleep, bathed in a new light.

WHY DID I like Frog? First and foremost because he had declared he loved me, and with that, he moved my earth and changed my place in the universe. Sometimes he waited for me after school, and as he walked me home I ascended into the clouds, higher and higher. Second, I liked him because he was independent, on his own. He had no parents to report to or to size me up. Home was a farm in the sticks with four brothers, assorted women, dogs, and cats. Something off an Allman Brothers album.

Meanwhile, my mother was raised to a new level of fretting. The pressure on her barely beating heart! Without my father, she was grasping for reasons to live and having to deal with me. She knew I was headed for trouble but couldn't pronounce how deeply.

She knocked on my door while I was busy fraying a pair of jeans.

"Marcy?"

"Hi, Mom."

"What on earth you are doing to good pants?"

"Making them look cool."

She shook her grave head while I held them up to make sure they were ratty enough.

"Mrs. Duncan call."

"Oh," I said guiltily.

"She say she sorry you are fired."

I kept on fraying.

"Because of bad boy you are fired?"

"He had nothing to do with it. And he's not bad. Not really."

"He bad boy. I see him outside house. If he come to door, I make you call police."

"Why is everyone against me? Why can't I have some fun?"

"Fun not part of life, Marcy. That dangerous way to think. You think Daddy grow up having fun? He starving to death! If he only think about fun, you are starve to death, too."

"I'd rather starve to death than not have any fun!"

"Fun more important than help Tim and Tom? Fun more important than write letter to Daddy?" she said, shoving a postcard in my face.

"Yes!" I cried out of pure defiance.

She looked at me long and hard like I had just proved to her what she had known all along: I wasn't worthy enough to be her daughter.

A SMILING Indonesian boy was sitting atop an ox while three boys looked on in a parched-looking field on this postcard. They were described as *Farmer's children enjoying their companion.*

My darling Marcy,

I had a busy day today. Meetings and meetings and more meetings. Afterwards, I was invited to a cocktail party at the house of a Japanese World Bank staff member. He is American born but his wife is Japanese born. Although our countries' histories are poor, I try not to harbor any resentment, though I am the first to admit I am not perfect and would not like for them to read my thoughts, at times. It was a stuffy affair but for my meeting with an American World Bank staffer who said upon our introduction—"So you're the famous economist Mr. Moon!" What did he mean by that? Perhaps he had one too many scotches!

I have not received word from you in several days now and am growing a tad bit worried. Don't forget your dear old pop just because he isn't home with you. The man of the family has to make a living, even if it is a tiresome one.

Love, Dad

P.S. Please tell Owen my dinosaur bones thank him for digging the ditch for me. I wonder if he could put some soil or sand under the concrete slab of the front porch so that we don't have to worry about basement leakage.

15

B Y S U P P E R T I M E , we settle in. Except for wrapping her in an Indian blanket and fitting her with tiny coral-colored moccasins, Pablo has not parted with June Moon. To all gods, he has claimed her. They're on the back porch right now, swinging as one, watching the last bit of light sink into dusk. Pablo has forgotten how she got here, he's too busy singing, *"June Moon, you saw me standing alone..."*

Luke has fallen asleep on the couch, his bed from here on out. When his eyes are closed, he looks more Asian, though the gold in his hair and his lanky frame give his divided heritage away. He claimed he was tired from the bus ride, but the truth is, his bones are settling his soul down. All signs of Suicide Spell have vanished from his face.

Cactus Bear.

Our quarters are furnished with Cactus Bear second-hand stuff. Nothing matches but it all comes together like an old quilt. Everything's worn and torn, brought back to life with our touch, and now Luke's and June Moon's. Hand-to-heart art.

"Soup's on!" I call out.

No one stirs.

"I t ' s   n o t Rodeo Drive but what do you think of the shop, Luke?" Pablo asks.

"You have tons of turquoise stuff," Luke notes.

"The jewel of the desert," I say.

"The beaded necklaces are cool," Luke says. "There's a store on the pier that sells them but they're plastic."

"You won't find plastic in Cactus Bear," I say.

"Amen," Pablo agrees.

"Not even credit cards," I add.

"Amen!" Pablo agrees.

"Maybe I'll get one for my mom," Luke says. "She likes neck-laces."

"I think it might clash with her wardrobe," I say. "Beads aren't her style."

Pablo changes the subject. "How's the soup, Luke?"

He nods. "Pretty good."

"Pablo made this batch," I say.

"It's better than yours, Marcy. No offense," Luke says.

"I like to add salsa and herbs," Pablo says. "It gives it zip."

"And zing," Luke says.

"And zest!" Pablo says. "What did I tell you, Marcy? You make your soup so bland I start dreaming of oatmeal."

"You want spicy, go back to L.A.," I jokingly retort.

"You're from L.A.?" Luke asks, amazed.

"Yup."

"Why did you come here?"

"The land of sunshine turned into the land of hell for Pablo," I say.

"Let me tell my own story," he says, squeezing my hand.

"The floor's all yours," I say, squeezing back.

"Well, I had what I thought was the ultimate life. I was a tax attorney and had it made. *It* being money."

"What's wrong with money?" Luke questions him. "Without it, you're a bum."

"No, no, that's where you're wrong, Luke. Look at Marcy here. She has no money. And certainly she's no bum."

"Thank you, Pablo."

"Anyway, for years I worked sixteen-hour days and didn't even stop to smell the cacti, do you know what I mean? One day I was driving to a client's when I realized I couldn't move my neck to see the traffic next to me. There were no signs leading up to it. I hated every minute of every hour of my life, but hey, I was making money. But now my neck was in crushing pain. Eventually it spread down to my shoulders and back. The only thing I could think about was quitting my job and becoming a beach bum. One day I was saying good-bye to the folks at the the Hanguk Home, a client of mine. Marcy was there saying good-bye to her mother. Wow, what a parallel. Anyway, I was about to pop another Valium when Marcy took my arm and said, "Don't take that pill, you ill idiot." Her gesture of kindness touched me. Up until then, my life was nothing but phone calls and portfolios and hustling on the freeway. I was going so fast only a woman like Marcy—a woman who saw the telling signs, not the dollar signs—could slow me down. We walked out of there together and I have never looked back."

"That part is only half true, Pablo. You do look back," I say.

"Less and less so," he says.

WHEN PABLO jerks in his sleep, he's reliving the pen-poking incident. He'll wake up jumpy the next morning. Any sudden movement and he'll karate-chop the air.

Poor Pablo! His split self secretly tears him apart. How can he find true bliss here when the highs of L.A. still call him? Can't he see? A double espresso would kill his tea-brewing talent. A five-star meal would ruin the soulful skill of his soup making. When he's not looking, the buzz in the back of his brain just might drown out the sound of chimes.

He's here forever, he's going back.

If I could focus hard enough on Pablo, I could predict which one he will eventually abandon, L.A. or Cactus Bear. The demon or the dream. But when I look into his eyes for clues, his self splits. One eye stares at me with more poetry than the night sky while the other drifts back to L.A.

AFTER SUPPER I go out for a walk, break my moccasins back in. They have sorely missed this path. My love for White Sky is an almost painful longing, so primitive it hurts. I belong here. I belong to the purplish light that breaks through the sky at this hour and I belong to the souls of the sagebrush. I belong to an ancient wonder for which there are no words.

Once I'm back at Cactus Bear, the wonder is gone. Luke is talking to Cleo on the phone. The chimes signal my entrance; he hands me the phone.

"Mom wants to talk to you," he says.

With dread, I say, "Hello, Cleo."

"I can't believe you did this, Marcy! I called the house at least a hundred times tonight! What on God's earth were you thinking?"

"That your children would enjoy my home."

"Without my permission?"

"Would you have given it?"

"That's not the point! Here I am, across the country, on the brink of unveiling my product to the international food industry, and I have to worry about my children being abducted into some desert hovel! I can't believe you did this! I absolutely can't believe it!"

I speak so low Luke can't hear me. "You didn't worry about them in San Francisco. You only worried about yourself and your damn company."

"That's a fucking lie! Do you realize you're accusing me of not loving my children?"

"If you love your children so much, why are you in New York?"

"Marcy," she says, "I don't know what's happened to you. To us. But my head is on the brink of explosion. I'm trying very hard not to overreact. After the show is over, I'm flying in and taking my kids home. Do you understand?"

"I understand," I lie.

THE CHIMES sound, a couple wander in looking for hand-carved whistles. Luke shows them the way, down an aisle of engraved pottery bottles. The couple purchase two whistles along with a decorated water jug.

"What's my commission?" Luke asks with good humor after they leave.

I lead Luke to our moccasin rack. We sell everyday moccasins and special-occasion moccasins. Plain tan moccasins and tricolored beaded moccasins. The sign above reads *Mo' Moccasins*.

"Take your pick," I say.

He tries on several pairs.

"Luke, did you call your mom or did she call you?"

"I called. Pablo said I could."

"Of course you can call her. Anytime."

He settles for a blue pair with red and yellow beading.

"These are rain-dance moccasins, Luke. During a drought you can wear them and call upon the rain gods."

"Every day's a drought around here," he comments. "Should I wear them every day?"

"No, don't abuse them. These are special-occasion moccasins. According to White Sky legend, if it rains in the desert while you're wearing your moccasins, it's a sign of your positive powers."

"I just want them as a souvenir," he says.

. . .

THE CHIMES are going crazy tonight. Luke and I take care of our customers one by one. I roll out a rug, he steers a lady to the candle section. I bag a shawl, he packs up a set of mugs. Pablo and June Moon are upstairs in sweet Nevada heaven. If Cleo could see this, maybe she'd get lost and leave us alone.

"How do all these people know about Cactus Bear in the middle of nowhere?" Luke wonders. "It's not like there's a Blockbuster next door."

"Word of mouth goes a long way in the desert. Not that we don't have our double-digit dead days."

"What's a double-digit dead day?"

"A day when we ring up under a hundred dollars."

"We sold more than that tonight!" he proudly points out.

We high-five.

"I couldn't have done it without you," I say. "We're a team, Luke. Partners."

He surveys Cactus Bear with new appreciation. "There's so much cool stuff here. Where do you find it?"

"It finds us," I explain. "All good things come to Cactus Bear."

A HALF hour without a customer and Luke defaults to his old self, the boy bored stiff in San Francisco. I have an idea.

Luke watches me set out my Paduk board and two bowls of stones at a coffee table covered with dog bites. Pablo and I love this table; eat at it, read at it, kick it around. Every nick adds to its charm.

Luke grins. "Is this some New Age game?"

"Actually, it's an Old Age Korean game called Omok. I used to play it as a kid."

"Did my mom play?"

"Not too often. She didn't like it."

He grins again. "You mean she didn't like losing."

I turn down the lights and light a candle. In this flickering state I explain the ancient rules of Omok to a modern-day boy. He is more attentive than I thought possible. He studies the board, its grids; his eyes open with life, some meaning beyond. Outside, the wind blows; inside, Luke juggles black stones back and forth in his palms.

We play.

I always beat Pablo at Omok. He's so torn apart he plays with only a half-hearted attempt. But Luke plays with his whole broken heart. And when he wins, he declares, "Omok!"

L i k e   w h i t e and black stones, Luke and I are moving toward each other. It feels like more than a game. It feels like our destiny.

" L u k e ,   l e t ' s play another game," I suggest.

"Like what?"

"Expression."

"Omok!" he declares again.

"How about it?"

"No, but you go ahead. You can talk about your dad, if you want."

So I do. "My dad used to say, 'When I need hope, I look up at the sun. The sun makes the grapes grow on vines. And the sun turns grapes into raisins. The sun is a miracle worker. It has saved me from darkness.' My dad cherished Sunmaid raisins. As a hungry child, he believed the sun maiden was Jesus. The Sunmaid raisin box became his Bible, his vision. His hope in a sea of filthy water. He would end up living with the concept of looking up to the sun his whole life, even as a full-grown man."

The phone cuts me off with a rude ring. It's Cleo, hallucinating in New York.

"What about this Pablo character? He's not going to molest my children, is he?"

ONLY CLEO could come up with that. Only Cleopatra Moon. Yes, I recognize the voice after all these years. Oh, it's calmer, it's cooler, less cursing allowed. But the bottled-up hatred still seeps out of every perfumed pore of her body. How dare she accuse Pablo! He came out to the desert to remember how to dream. He came out here to quiet his fires.

Not all his fires, though. Pablo is a deeply passionate but understanding man. He knows when and how he can touch me and when and how he can't. What he doesn't know is why. He has questioned me, gently, so many times I could scream like I screamed that one fateful summer day.

16

I HOPPED ON Frog's moped and we were off to Rainbow Run, a creek on the fringe of western Fairfax County. It was known to me only as a getaway in the boonies, the home of keg parties—certainly no destination of mine. To get there, we flew over bumpy country roads. My arms were around Frog's waist, my jeans were fraying in the wind, my Berry Cherry lips were so glossy they blinded the birds. I could never, not in my wildest, most fiery dreams, invent a moment more charged than this. This put cruising with Cleo to shame. This defined every sweet rock 'n' roll lyric ever sung. I was part of the plan now, to be young and flying in the face of fear under an endless blue sky that promised to go on forever. Frog's voice was gravel as we took a steep bend: "Hang on tight, Miss Moonface!"

We flew over potholes and bumps and dead squirrels, never looking back. In a frenzy of moving fences and abandoned lots, I squeezed into the flesh of this shaggy rebel with startling ease.

Around Frog, harm could come my way, but I was willing to pay the price.

When we got to Rainbow Run, we wiped out on a dirt trail. I saw sky and pebbles and water so glittery I must have been dreaming. Frog wasn't phased.

"We're here!" he announced.

"Cool," I said.

He gave me a hand until we were eye to eye. We said nothing, the silence spoke for itself. Overcome, he ran his hands freely over my body.

I jumped. "Stop it."

"Just brushing the shit off you."

"I said, stop it!"

He held me close and breathed in my ear with an insolence that gave me goose bumps. "Can't."

"Frog?"

"Huh?" he nibbled.

"Let's talk."

"Man!" He fell apart, broke loose from me. "That's all we do! Talk, talk, talk until I'm blue in the face. I've got telephonitis, thanks to you. What's left to talk about?"

"Well "—I stalled—"like, what do you want to be when you grow up?"

"Me, only with my own place."

"Don't you like living with your brothers?"

"Naw, they fight too much. Whenever I tell them to shut up, they go, 'Any law against raising hell under your own roof?' When I tell them the house stinks of dope, they go, 'One more fucking peep out of you and your butt's out the door!'"

"You don't smoke dope?"

"Naw, it's wicked stuff. Don't drink, either. My brothers puke themselves to sleep seven days a week. I told myself when I was twelve, I was never going to be like that. And if I was, I'd clean up my own mess."

"Where are your parents?"

He shrugged. "Around."

"Around where?"

"This very minute, you mean? Who knows? They ditched us to go work on some farm in West Virginia that went belly up. Then they moved on."

"Don't they keep in touch with you?" I wondered.

"Hey, I don't read their letters and I don't take their calls. What's the point? They split. Didn't exactly leave me with no guardian angels."

He hurt, I could tell. Brooded on his trashed-out lot in life. But I wasn't at the age to offer comfort. It was, like so many things, beyond me. Splashes from the creek broke the somber spell.

"Want to go swimming?" I suggested.

He grinned. "I didn't bring you up here to go swimming."

Then he took my hand and led me to a shady spot under a maple tree. It was the most natural thing to do, crumbling under him onto the ground. In one swift move, his transistor radio emerged from his pocket and he tuned in Peter Frampton singing "Baby I love your way." Frog had a disheveled crawled-out-of-the-alley look about him, so the scent of strawberry musk in his hair surprised me as he bumped and boogied his way to our first kiss. It was heaven. I heard birds and partying and Frog crooning lyrics I had only crooned to myself. His vulgar expression and hungry lips wanted more of me so I closed my eyes, forgot who I was, and got into it, mind, body, and soul. It was like slipping into water. I was swimming, floating, coming up for air.

"I dig your Chinese face," he moaned.

"I'm not Chinese," I moaned back.

"Don't matter, I dig it anyway. Your eyes are black as night. Blacker, even. And you have the goddamnest, smallest, bite-sized mouth," he said, sinking into it.

"Frog, I can't breathe," I said. "Frog, get up!"

"Sorry," he said, lifting up, then rolling over on his back.

We faced the sky, wondering what was next.

He blinked. "Want a smoke?"

"I don't know how," I said.

Frog lit up and offered me a drag off his cigarette. I took it and puffed my heart out.

I HAD not written my father in two weeks, and my mother was well aware. Too aware. Her face shriveled with disgust when I walked into the kitchen, back from Rainbow Run. She was making a new batch of kimchi, as her last jar had gone sour from sitting too long on the windowsill. Did I look as different as I felt? My lips were swollen, but tingling. The earth was still moving. Whoever I was before was not ever coming back.

"Daddy postcard on your bed," she said.

.   .   .

THE POSTCARD pictured palm trees and other exotic vegetation on either side of a canal where people in straw hats rowed their canoes. I turned it over and read, *Dhonburi: Scene of the floating market.*

> *My darling Marcy,*
>
> *I know you are busy with the Duncan boys and advanced French in summer school, and that is all fine and dandy, but still you must squeeze perhaps ten minutes out of your hectic schedule to write your dear old dad who worries about you at any given moment. I am not, after all, having such a grand time overseas as some romantics would believe. My typical day consists of office meetings, field meetings, boring dinners with assorted diplomats and their wives (not all boring, but most), writing notes for future reports, sometimes until two or three a.m. I go to bed exhausted and wake up not particularly refreshed, as you know I suffer from poor sleep and jet lag. Plus, the foreign food often does not sit well in my stomach. And still I find the time to correspond with my family, who I hope worries about me, too, without Mommy's nutritious Korean meals and the smiles of my beautiful girls.*
>
> *I don't mean to sound too harsh, Marcy. I know you are a good girl, at an age of distraction. But as your father, am I not entitled to hear from you on a daily basis? Drop me a line!*
>
> *Love, Dad*
>
>
> *P.S. Another month has passed. Did you select another book from the Book of the Month Club? Do not let time lapse, or we will receive a dud.*

I put the postcard down and pulled out a blue airmail letter from my desk drawer. *Dear Dad*, I wrote, pondering an opening line. What do I say? What does he want to hear? He was right— I was at an age of distraction! Besides, if I put down on paper what I was really feeling, he would have the proof to disown me.

I stuck the blue airmail letter back in my desk.

EVERY DAY after summer school, Frog and I would scoot off to Rainbow Run. Frog was a daredevil, freewheeling in the path of honking cars, mooning death with a howl.

"My calling is to break all the rules, Miss Moonface!"

Once there, we'd go at it in view of any willing watchers and a sun so hot its memory is piercing. God was finally shining down on me! I fit into this blessed microcosm called earth. I was a worm, crawling out from under a rock. No, a tie-dyed butterfly, breaking out of its cocoon. As I lay beneath Frog moving and grooving to Stevie Wonder, what was I feeling besides being one with the earth? Something like heaven and golden lady and going there— Or was that just Frog serenading me, all lips?

Spurred by the song, he asked, "How about it, Miss Moonface? Would you go there with me?"

"Like where are you talking about?"

"Anywhere but here."

"What are you talking about?"

"I'm talking about blowing this boring burb. Making a break. Skipping town."

"You mean run away?"

"Miss Moonface got the message!" Frog hollered across Rainbow Run.

"Forget it. No way."

"Why not? Who would miss you? Your old lady's waiting for your old man to come home and your sister's a full-time bitch working overtime. Hang around here and you'll grow up to be a chick with no place to go."

"Shut up, you moron. Cleo's not a bitch."

"So why does she flip me off from her bedroom window?"

"She can flip off anyone she wants."

Frog sighed. "According to the Bitch's Bill of Rights, I guess."

He veered off the subject of Cleo and back onto his dreaming road. "Someday when I get a real bike, we'll split and go southwest. Arizona, New Mexico, Nevada. Ride through the desert at midnight with no one on our backs. The air will be cold and black and so quiet you can hear an ash drop."

FROG DREAMED of building a boat and sailing down to the Caribbean. He dreamed of bumming around Ocean City and rummaging through McDonald's garbage. He dreamed, too, of hiding in a shack way deep in the woods where no one could find him. His dreams were the dreams of a faceless hobo. Even then, I knew that. I also knew Frog was not part of my future. We weren't going anywhere together. Frog would end up in the gutter, despite his genius, which was vague and rambling but pervaded every word uttered from his smoky lips. Who cared? That summer he was the boy kissing me, eating away at my neck until it was raw meat, not caring if all his dreams died in my arms.

"We can't do this forever, Miss Moonface. Let's go all the way."

"Why?"

"Because."

"Because why?"

"Because it's only natural to want to get naked with a willing chick."

"Why do you have to talk that way, you jerk?"

"It's the only way I know how to talk, you sexy bitch."

"Well, who says I'm willing?"

"Your little wet tongue says it. Your little black eyes say it. Your bra-locked boobs say it," he said, fumbling with the buttons on my vest.

"Get your grubby hands off of me!"

This time Frog hollered, "Miss Moonface is a virgin!"

SO WAS Frog, I learned a moment later.

"But I've done it in my head so many times I could teach sex ed with my eyes closed. Plus, I've seen it firsthand. It's *Saturday Night Live* at the Fitzgerald Farm! My brothers do it dead drunk in their sleep on the couch with the closest chick at hand."

"You watched them?"

"It's a crowded house," he said, making no apologies.

A rapturous sex state came over him. He groaned like it hurt in a really good way.

"Your lips taste berry good but I want to taste something sweeter, Miss Moonface," he whispered. "Once we get started, you'll open up like a flower, swear to God and the angels, too. You'll feel like a flower, all pretty and perfumed with me inside of you."

"I don't know," I mumbled.

Frog knew I was wavering. Unsure of my footing on this earth. He got me up and led me to a spot in the woods far from the safe, splashing sounds of Rainbow Run. It was shady, damp, dangerous. When he set me down on the ground, twigs broke in my ears. He wrapped his arms and legs around me like vines, strangling me.

"I don't like it here," I said. "Let's go back."

"Uh-uh," he purred feverishly.

I bit his hand and managed to break away from him. He pinned me against a tree. Hot panic speared through me.

"Where do you think you're going?" he said.

"Let go of me."

But he couldn't stop himself. His hands were traveling freely under my vest, my T-shirt. He unhooked my bra and squeezed me with half-conscious moans. A moment of murder could not have been more terrifying. Both God and the devil heard my bloodcurdling scream: "Let go of me!"

"No can do." He panted and pushed until the wedge of light above me that crept between the trees was my only way out. Down here I was screaming but I zoned in on that light like it was all I had to hold on to, held on to it like a flame or a raisin so sweet I'd die before giving it up. Frog had his hand down my pants and split me wide open in a place so virginal not even a tampon had touched it. With a fistful of electrified fingers, he jammed away, moaning and drooling for dear sweet life. It hurt, it hurt, it hurt so much. At some point I stopped scream-ing, looked up at the light, and heard *I know you are a good girl, I know you are a good girl.* Up there, I was still alive. Down here I was dead. Frog stopped abruptly, flared his horny nostrils at me.

"It can be fun, you know."

I turned to stone and his hand wilted out of my pants.

"Man"—he shrugged—"you're lucky I like you."

Despite the sight of his blood-streaked fingers and the throb-bing between my legs, I held my head up, silently defiant.

"Come on! You're different. Most dudes don't dig Chinese chicks. My brothers told me to lay off the egg rolls and get my head examined!"

"I'm not a Chinese chick, you stupid hick," I said.

"It doesn't matter 'cause I dig you anyway. You've got a chance at love right here, right now. Let me prove it to you."

"Go to hell, you ignoramus anus."

"What did you call me?"

"You're nothing but an ignoramus anus. And you'll end up with a big fat pink Petunia in a white shack and your kids will wash their cooties off in the sprinkler."

"Man, what tongue are you talking?"

I slapped his face; sweat flew. He looked so stunned I slapped him again, this time so hard he lost his balance, bumped into a tree, saw stars.

"Korean!" I cried.

Then I abruptly turned and walked away with no notion of how I was getting home.

.   .   .

I HAVE no memory of hitchhiking home, only getting out at the curb, disoriented and yet...weirdly victorious. I had stood my ground, I had slapped Frog's ugly face. But once in the door, something happened to me. My soul sank and took my heart with it to the bottom of the sea. The light was gone, it seemed to me, and as my eyes explored, I saw that the curtains were drawn. Suddenly I knew I was about to fall out of one nightmare and into another.

My mother was at the kitchen table, hands crossed.

"Mom?"

She sat statue-still.

"Mom, what's wrong?"

"Daddy sick."

"How?"

"*Aigoo!*" she wailed.

"Mom, what's wrong?"

"*Aigoo, giga magida!*"

Cleo was home—her car was parked in the driveway—so I left my mother in her foreign frenzy and rushed into Cleo's room. She was on her knees, clutching postcards and mumbling prayers. Incense burned on her dresser.

"Somebody tell me what's going on," I cried. "What's happened to Dad?"

She finished her prayer with an exhaustive amen. Her face was streaked with tears.

"He's in a hospital in Hong Kong," she sobbed.

"What? Why?"

"He had like a nervous breakdown!"

A nervous breakdown? Meg had them left and right—when

her chin broke out in zits, when her brother borrowed her BeeGees album and gave it back scratched. But what was a real nervous breakdown?

"What does it mean, Cleo?"

"Marcy"—she cradled my head—"he tried to jump off a plane."

I was suffocating, falling out of my life, falling out of a plane.

"He was on a flight bound for Seoul when he had this, this panic attack. He just wanted off the plane. Exit one, two, three. Good-bye, world. He got up and began pounding on the door. Can you imagine Dad doing that? Pounding like some lunatic madman in front of total strangers? He wanted to go down into the South China Sea! When the plane stopped in Hong Kong, he got off and checked himself into a hospital. The doctors say he'll be okay. But will he? Will he really be okay?"

"Why did he want to jump off the plane, Cleo?"

She didn't respond, she was gagging on near death.

"Why did he want to jump off the plane?" I repeated.

"Because he wants out!"

CLEO ENGAGED me in prayer, on our knees, on the floor. All the bad blood between us went up like incense. We were two flames, burning as one.

"Dear God, give Dad his strength back. Help him get over this crisis. Bless his destroyed, sick spirit. If You help him get well, we'll give up our rotten ways. I'll go back to school. I'll be-come a born-again virgin. And Marcy won't go out with that punk again," Cleo promised.

"I won't, God," I promised.

"Just help Dad get well. Please, please, please. He's the only father we have!"

"Amen," we said.

ALL THE while I was picturing my father, halfway around the globe, pale and paralyzed in a hospital room. I shuddered and couldn't stop. How could this be the same man for whom juggling four ice-cream cones back to the car from High's Dairy made his whole day? The sky was starry, our windows were cracked open. Something about that whole simple scene made him happy. The family, waiting in the car.

Ice-cream, an American dream.

But right now that scene was so far away. It was the dimmest star in the universe.

If only I could bring my father a box of Sunmaid raisins. I didn't need to see him—could I even face him?—but I could just slip in and out, leaving the box by his bedside. Then, when he awoke, the young boy in him would resurrect himself with hope, and eat the nourishing raisins one by one. If he had a sunny room, the vision of his Sunmaid Jesus would fill his eyes. Surely this would save him from the dark waters that called him. Surely this would bring him back to life.

SOMETIME THAT evening my mother put her beloved deck of cards away.

What did this mean? Solitaire had defined her. The fixture

on the kitchen counter my whole life was suddenly missing. I watched her gnaw on the same stringy piece of *toraji* during our silent supper, and knew why. Her will to play was like her appetite. Gone.

"Mom, can I go to Hong Kong?"

"How you gonna go?"

"Fly."

"Where your wings?"

"No, I mean by airplane."

"How you pay?"

"I'll pay you back."

"How? You stop teaching Duncan boys, spend all money on makeup, not Mind of Peace. You think money grow on bushes? Beside, what good you are doing in Hong Kong? Daddy never come home if he see you now, he stay in hospital bed cover over head. Blame me you wear cheap clothes, have bites all over neck. He probably sick to death because you don't write him letter. Bad daughter!"

C L E O   H A D called it our rotten ways, but I now believe my father would have forgiven me and blamed it not on my mother or me but on what he had coined that age of distraction. But that night in my room, all I knew was that I hated myself. My soul was no good. Over and over I read the postcard from my father that had arrived for me that day.

The postcard was of dingy wooden houses on the water and peasant people selling food from their canoes. It read, *Here shows the riverside houses where the sub-canal separated.*

My darling Marcy,

Thailand is an awfully hot and sticky place. When you have a mountain of work to do, it is an interference. I'm sure it is just a matter of getting used to it. On second thought, the locals don't look particularly comfortable. All day long they fan themselves, waiting for a breeze that never seems to come.

Guess what, Marcy? I find myself humming your song, "Why Am I Always Waiting?" in the shower, in taxis, even while I am writing this. It is my way of thinking of you. The song has a very pleasant melody, even for an old fogey like myself. That you have so many interests pleases me. Song writing, French, teaching, etc. One day you must narrow it down to one subject and shoot for the moon. Although you are a talented and smart girl, you must always try to be number one. Oriental people in America are like Avis rental cars. We're number two—we have to try harder. By that I don't mean we are second-class citizens, but in the eyes of so-called "real" Americans, we have to prove ourselves equal. For your own good, don't question this too deeply. (Of course, you and Cleo and Mommy are all number one in my book!)

Why haven't you been writing? I hope to find a letter from you when I arrive at the Singapura Hotel. I have been away so long I may not recognize you at the airport.

Love, Dad

I couldn't sleep. Too much had happened. I got up and turned on my globe. It lit up like a candle in my room. My eyes zeroed in on Hong Kong. Something I can only call my father's future ghost materialized next to me. In this safe and comforting dimension, our auras touched.

At night you can light it up, Marcy, and dream of traveling, as I did when I was your age. Of course, the only globe I owned was in my head. But maybe that made the dream bigger, more visible....

And then, too soon, he was gone.

I opened my desk drawer and sifted through all my postcards, rereading them by the light of the globe. I was looking for something, I had no idea what. Something that would help me understand why on earth my father wanted to jump off a plane.

My darling Marcy,

I am writing this postcard from a 747, moments before nodding off. I arrived on the airplane in poor spirits, as it was delayed for three hours. Not that that is so unusual but I was in a sour mood to begin with. Once I was on board they served Champagne which almost immediately made me feel good. The grouchiness went away in no time, floated away like bubbles. Then the magnificent French cuisine was served. It was well worth the three-hour wait. I put aside the dieting guilt for the night and devoured everything that was served to me. Smoked salmon, salad with French dressing, the chicken dish called coq au vin, white wine, a variety of cheese, tea and liqueur. It was a meal fit for a king. I was content. No longer angry.

When you are an adult, surely you will experience many fine first-class meals like this and remember how good it is to be alive.

*Write me at the Erawan Hotel in Bangkok. Mommy has
the address.*

Love, Dad

I recognized this voice. This was the voice of the man who
would force his way into heaven from a funk until he would see
life through the artificial glow of a globe, a good meal, a glass of
Champagne. Then all was perfect in the world.

I had heard this voice all my life, but tonight it sounded in
my ears like a death drum, louder and louder. For the first time
in my fourteen years, I could read between the lines and understand that such soaring states could only come from a man who
was drowning in pain.

17

THE PEACEFUL pace of Cactus Bear is disrupted by Cleo's calls, day and night. We have spoken more in the past few days than in the past twenty years. But these are not cherished conversations. *What were you thinking? Have you lost your mind? I still can't believe this is happening! Do you swear Pablo's not some one-eyed wacko?*

"He can't even see straight—how can he take care of June Moon? He'll drop her on some goddamn prickly cactus. Or *his* prick. Keep Luke away from him, too."

"Don't you have a food show to run?"

"Where do my children sleep? On some smelly bear rug?"

"Luke gets the couch, June Moon sleeps between Pablo and me," I say.

It would be a waste of breath to tell her that when everyone falls asleep, the spirits dance over the desert to the echoes of our beating hearts.

"Does Pablo have a record?"

I liken Cleo's loss of composure to a mummy unraveling and rotting. Now, that's smelly! What's underneath is who she is minus the wraps of a million-dollar home and million-dollar looks. What's underneath is her darkness, exposed.

YET THIS I cannot deny: I feel myself floating back down to earth, floating like a feather toward an unceremonious reality: Cleo is taking the children home.

ON WEDNESDAY morning, one day before the Moccathon, I confront Luke, who's inspecting our collection of magic crystals and stones set on blue velvet in a scratched Plexiglas case. We call it our magic case.

"Luke, do you like it here?"

He nods, mesmerized. "How can these be magic?"

"If you believe they are, then they are."

"Do you believe they are?"

"Yes, I do. I absolutely do."

"So I could hold a magic stone in my hands and make a wish come true? Is that how it works?" he wonders.

"Do you want to?"

"I'm just asking."

"Because the power lies within you. You can make anything happen. What do you wish would happen, Luke?"

He shrugs. "Nothing."

We stare into the magic case.

My heart nearly explodes when I say these words: "If you could live here, would you like that?"

He shakes his sad, clouded head. "It's not my home."

"Home is where the sun and moon hang over your roof. Home is a bed worn down by dreams, Luke."

"San Francisco is my home. But like I said, I like it here enough."

More than anything, I wish Luke would break into a great big smile. A smile without any reservation. His aura is still dark; it does not catch the sun, it eclipses the moon. If he would just smile for me, I could let him go back with Cleo and not feel our flames go out.

"Have you given any thought to the Moccathon?" I ask.

"Walking doesn't bother me. I'll walk with you," he offers.

We squint through scratched Plexiglas while the crystals and stones do their thing.

"We'll walk together, Luke. We'll walk for miles, we'll touch the horizon, we'll keep on walking until we see what's on the other side."

NOT LITERALLY, I know that. I know I am walking the Moccathon so that the White Sky will have the funds to open an herbal healing clinic. But somewhere in the back of my mind, where it's foggy and hard to get to, I believe I will break some time barrier on that walk. After that, it's all a blank.

.   .   .

THE AFTERNOON is long, slow, nearly chimeless in Cactus Bear—I have taken the phone off the hook. Every hour is sun-drenched heaven. Luke is roaming the desert as every loner should, taking a breather from ten straight games of Omok. We're pretty evenly matched, though he's got a couple of games on me. Pablo and I alternate holding June Moon while the other tends to the occasional customer. Even Pablo has let go a little, of June Moon and the dream, and something about the whole situation suddenly exhausts him, jolts him, when she's in my arms.

"Are we ever going to do it, Marcy?"

"Do what?"

"Adopt a White Sky baby."

"Someday," I say.

"No, not someday," he says testily. "I want to get married today and adopt a baby tomorrow."

"Whoa, there."

"No. I've been doing that for four long years. I want an answer and I want it now."

"An ultimatum? I don't believe my ears."

"Believe them."

"I don't know who I'm talking to. June Moon, do you know who I'm talking to? Do you recognize this voice in the room? Funny, neither do I!"

"Here I am in Cactus Bear in White Sky, Nevada, with a woman who will only sleep with me once in a blue moon—pun intended. Four years of Expression and not a clue about why; I'll probably be in the dark for the rest of my life. Okay, I accept that, reluctantly. We meditate instead of make love. But give me something to hold on to; tell me that something I want will be. I take back what I said earlier; it doesn't have to be today or tomorrow. I'm just asking for a little hope here, just a little look that means yes. I never got that. I wanted to write plays but my father forbade that, said I'd die in the gutter with nothing left to say. So I went for the big bucks and I let my clients run my life. I did things to please them, put my butt on the line so the zillionaires wouldn't pay a penny in taxes. Nothing was for me, ever."

"Let it go, Pablo. Please."

"I'm tired of letting it go! I even let one son of a bitch blind me, and I just stared back at him. Didn't even sue him; you know, an eye for an eye. Sure, there's a lot I love here—the mind-numbing silence and the slow motion of things—but if I can't ask for something and get it, then nothing's changed for me. I can eat soup and donate my life to the needy but if *my* needs aren't fulfilled, if they're treated like the bottom of the pot, then I'm still the sorry bastard I was in L.A."

"Don't let me stand in your way. If you want to go back to L.A., go," I say.

"How can you say that?"

"Because a part of you wants to go."

"That's crazy! You're being insecure. I love you. You know that."

"Then why do you sublet your apartment? Why haven't you given up the lease? You say you love me but you've got one foot out the door."

"No I don't!"

"Admit it, Pablo, you're not committed to this life past today. So quit accusing me of your crime."

"Like you are? At least I mingle with the locals, make friends, get involved. But to you, it's all theory. You want to save the White Sky but who do you know? Do you have a single White Sky friend? And don't say Ned—he's just the moccasin maker to you."

"I know them in spirit. I know their ancestors," I declare.

"That's bull, Marcy. Your Moccathon has zilch to do with the White Sky or an herbal healing clinic. I've never even heard you say one decent thing about an herb. Somehow, I'm not sure how, it's all wrapped up with your dad. Maybe because you stopped sending money to Sweet Charity when you were a girl and you still feel guilty about it. Which is sweet and honorable but destructive, too."

"It was called Peace of Mind, not Sweet Charity. And I drink herbal tea, don't I?"

"You're still married to the memory of your father, to the memory of when you were just a girl," Pablo insists. "But you're not a girl anymore. You've got to grow up and have your own family. Let it go, Marcy."

BY NIGHTFALL what Pablo said sinks into me, sinks like rainwater into desert ground. I hold my head up high. I know what I must do.

I KEEP it in our bedroom closet in a big box simply marked GLOBE. I take it out in moments of prayer and self-question and also on July 17, the date of my father's birth, and on October 9, the date of his death. Pablo knows when I get out my globe, it's time for him to turn off the light and leave the room. Now is one of those times.

But this time is not like the other times.

When I switch my globe on, it occurs to me that in all these years I have never once had to change the bulb. This light is the same light that illuminated our faces—mine and my father's— once. The thought both comforts and saddens me.

I gaze into my globe and wish what I said to Luke was true. That if I believed it was magic, then it was magic, a great big magic crystal ball. I could spin it and go back in time to the summer my sister was Cleopatra Moon. If I could be that girl back then, a Miss American Teen wannabe, I might believe it was magic.

You can dream on for a lifetime, li'l one. Dream on, dream on, dream on!

But did I dream on? No. And I didn't win the contest, either.

My fingers move over all the places my father visited. Singapore, New Zealand, Mexico, the Philippines, Thailand, France, all of South America. So many countries. He traveled the world, zoomed in and out of airports, rubbed elbows with dignitaries at cocktail parties and late-night dinners, then wrote reports until all hours. But in some ways, that sophisticated man of the world was not my father. My father was the man who would trudge downstairs and sink into grief late at night. On a wave of recovery, he was the man who took walks with his timer, trying to beat his own record.

I'm like an Avis car. I'm number two—I have to try harder!

My finger circles Korea, then lands on an unmarked mountainous village outside of Seoul where my father was born on the dirt floor of a church in the year 1923. I went there with him once on a hot, fragrant day. He picked a clutch of wild grass and asked me to hold on to it for safekeeping. When we got back to Glover he glued the grass to a sheet of paper and wrote *Yong Pyong* underneath it in both English and Korean. Then he framed it and hung it in his den. What was going through his mind when he looked at it? Why did he care? My mother has the only photograph of him as a child, aged four, dressed in an outfit made for a child half his size. His head was large and his eyes were empty. I take my globe in my hands and hold it until they grow warm, so warm.

I do this for a long time.

One last time I spin my globe. His presence is so real I can feel his face, so close it almost touches mine. We are two lost souls, parting.

You are a good girl, Marcy. A smart girl. I am going to miss you.

Must you leave now?

Yah.

Forever?

Yah.

My finger trembles on the switch. Every molecule in me breaks down. I know what I must do. Just before I do it, just before the room goes black, I say, "Bye, Dad."

I COME to the supper table, composed now, a woman on the brink of making Moccathon history. Pablo has baked a loaf of brown bread to dunk in our soup tonight. The loaf is warm and studded with seeds to fortify us for our long walk tomorrow. Pablo isn't walking—it's not his one-eyed vision, he says.

"Where's the butter?" Luke laughs, knowing better.

"You don't need butter, Luke. The molasses makes it rich and moist," Pablo says.

Luke agrees. "It's good. Real good."

We eat.

THE CHIMES have been eerily still tonight. Luke and I pass the time playing Omok. Pablo is upstairs reading to June Moon.

"Omok!" Luke cries.

"Luke?"

He looks up.

"I have something for you."

I go upstairs and get my globe. Pablo sees me and puts his book down.

"Marcy, what are you doing?"

"Not now, Pablo. Not now."

I HOLD it up like a trophy. "I want you to have this, Luke."

He looks at me with young confusion. "Why?"

"Because I want you to have it, that's why."

"But your dad gave it to you. It's yours."

"But now I want to give it to you. I've never given you anything in your whole life. I've never sent you a birthday card or a Christmas present. I've never been any kind of aunt to you. So please accept this. I know it may look like an ordinary globe, and I know you can call one up on your computer screen, but this one is special. It was a gift from my father—your grandfather—to me. Now I'm passing it on to you."

"But do you think your dad would have wanted me to have it? I mean, do you think he would have liked me?"

"Liked you? Luke, he would have loved you. He would have cherished the ground you walked on. He would have put you on a pedestal so high your head would be spinning in the clouds. He would have been honored to pass it on to you himself. He never had a son and it's a big deal in Korea—first son. But you would have been first grandson and that would have suited him just fine. Beyond that, Luke, you're an amazing person. I'm not just saying that, either. You're thoughtful, introspective, and so darn smart it scares me. You're bothered, true, your heart is damaged, but someday you'll let go and open up and reach a state of Cactus Bear you never thought possible."

Luke stares at the Paduk board, speechless. His face is so serious. What is he thinking?

"Marcy?"

"Yes?"

"I want to play the game."

"Okay." I hold my breath. "Which game?"

"Expression."

"Okay. Go ahead."

"You go first."

"No, Luke. It's your turn now."

He fidgets, sets down a black stone like we're back to playing Omok. With one move I clear the stone from the board.

"Game's over, Luke. You've got three minutes."

He sighs like every bone in his body is breaking. Slowly, tortuously, he opens up. When he speaks his lips quiver. "Stu had a girlfriend from the health club. Her name was Julia, she worked there. I saw them together and he saw me. He begged me not to tell my mom. He said he wouldn't see Julia anymore if I just didn't say anything. 'This is our secret, Luke. Telling your mother won't solve anything, it will only hurt her. I love your mother, I just made a mistake.' He begged me so long and hard I believed him. So I didn't say anything to my mom and tried not to think about it. But then I saw them together again, fooling around in the parking lot in broad daylight. I was so mad I started wishing Stu was dead. I wanted him to die for being a cheater and a liar. I thought about him dying all kinds of ugly deaths. And then he died. I wanted him to die and then he did. It's like I killed him."

"No, Luke. Don't think like that for one second. You didn't kill Stu. It was an accident. Do you understand?"

"Maybe I'm magic like the stones. Maybe I made it happen."

"No. It was an accident."

"I don't care if it was or wasn't. I'm glad he's dead!" he angrily shouts.

I grab Luke's shoulders and realize that every bone in his body *is* broken.

I hold him, wishing he were mine.

. . .

"WE NEED to talk," Pablo says.

We're in bed. June Moon is sleeping soundly between us. The hour is late. Our windows are open, the desert is so still I'm afraid to breathe and ruin the picture.

"Pablo, can we talk about us another time?"

"This has nothing to do with us. This is strictly you. Your sister is coming to town tomorrow and I think it's time you looked deep inside yourself."

"How deep?"

"As deep as the ocean in you."

"I'm looking," I say.

"And ask yourself why you would think for even a fraction of a second that Cleo caused the crash that killed her husband. Being a wild girl once or a selfish, money-oriented mother today is a far cry from being a murderer. A lot of people go through wild stages and a lot of people are selfish and money-oriented, Marcy. But they don't murder."

"She's a lousy mother and she was a lousy sister."

"That doesn't make her a murderer."

"I keep telling you, you don't know the whole story."

"Apparently not. But you've built *this* story out of thin air," Pablo says as he stretches over June Moon to kiss me good night. "Now I'm begging you, ask yourself why."

18

THEN WORD came from across the continents. My father was coming home! My mother was dancing, laughing, singing: "Daddy coming home in five days!"

I got hugs and kisses out of nowhere. They weren't meant for me, but I needed them. My experience with Frog was a bullet lodged in my brain. Yes, I hurt down there, too tender to touch, but thank God I didn't know then that it would throb for years, and that whenever my period came, an irrational fear would bleed in my brain, that Frog's fingers had somehow broken through long-gone scabs when I was asleep, or drugged. But right now I set the wound aside. All that mattered was my father's homecoming. All other trivia flew out some airplane window. *American Teen* magazine, two years of back issues. A dumb "Dream On" contest. The Song of the Century. Berry Cherry lip gloss.

What had really happened to my father was beyond my realm of understanding. He wanted to jump off a plane.

But he was recovered now, right?

"WRONG!" CLEO wailed, stirring ginger and scallions into a small bowl of soy sauce. "All it means is that he's functional, for now. Not in a hospital. But not well in the head, either. It could happen again. We have to watch him like hawks. Otherwise, bam! It could all be over. Next time"—she was adding pepper and stirring madly now—"it might be a bridge or a building."

"What are we watching for, Cleo?"

She hissed, chanted, cursed the devil with her soy-sauce potion. "Signs. Signs!"

"What kind of signs?"

She gave the bowl one final stir, then stopped with exhaustion.

"I'm not sure, li'l one."

LEGEND IN the Moon family was that my mother gave up the piano in a previous life in North Korea, that cold, remote, black spot on the globe. But now the whole house filled with song. A familiar song. *My* song! I hesitated on my way downstairs.

At the piano her face was radiant; she was transformed into the pupil in Sunchun with perfect posture, erect and obedient.

Her piano playing was far better than my father's slapstick attempts. Was it possible she had been playing in her head, all these years?

"Best song, Marcy!" she was singing. "I get telegram from Daddy. He say your song bring him back to life in hospital. He lying in bed and hear your song. *Your* song." She punctuated on the keyboard. "Best song in world. Make everyone happy. We sing together, okay?"

We sang our sad hearts out.

"Why am I always waiting?
Are the dreams I dream for real?
My mind is now debating
Over images I feel."

"You save Daddy's life." She embraced me. "We sing again!"

C L E O   A N D   I were driving back from the Korean store the day before my father's arrival. My mother had sent us there with a list of his favorite snacks—jelly candy, seaweed leaves, and dried fish. Now a pungent bag bloomed in the back seat. It was late afternoon, still blindingly sunny, but even in Cleo's Mustang we were just driving, not cruising. Our earlier friction went out that elusive airplane window and now we were bonded by my father's close brush with death. In fact, after it happened, Cleo quit her job on the spot and dusted Owen away.

"Cleo," I nervously blurted.

"Yeah?"

"I have something to tell you."

She turned off the radio and zoomed in on me, with her, in this car. "What is it?"

"Frog attacked me."

Cleo slowed down to a near halt while cars honked behind us. She flipped them off, then took my hand.

"Details," she said.

"He took me in the woods and put his hand down my pants." As the words spilled out of me, I regretted my whole life.

"He put his filthy hand down your pants." She quietly smoked. Not on a cigarette but something much more deadly. Nineteen years of rage. "Marcy, did he rape you?"

"No. He just kept pushing his fingers in and out of me, over and over. It really hurt a lot. I was bleeding."

"Oh my God," Cleo breathed.

She stripped the gears and screeched into eighty miles per hour.

"I'm going to fucking kill that ugly little sonovabitch punk!"

"Slow down, Cleo!" I cried.

She was smoking up a storm now. Fury spewed from her nostrils while she blasted the godforsaken sky. "He just wanted to see if you slanted up!"

"If what slanted up?"

"Oh my God, you don't know anything, do you? You're so naïve, so pure. How could you let that gross-out untouchable touch you with his grease-monkey paws? His kind—and all white bastards—talk about our kind and not in the most flowery terms. We're just a bet at the card table."

"What do they bet on?"

"On our cunts being as slanted as our eyes! The more per-verted ones try to find out."

I sank into the seat, sank below the dash, while Cleo contin-ued ranting about Leonard Lewandowski, every Petunia pig in the dorm, the damn doctor who punctured her on purpose.

"Even that Nurse Yanofsky can go to hell—if she'll fit. Here I thought she was okay but she was just an overgrown Petunia sending me flowers so I wouldn't sue her blubber butt for not giving me a shot of antibiotics! Somebody give *her* a shot of testosterone so the transformation will be complete!

"And Owen, good old boy Owen. Ha, ha, ha! You thought he was too good to be true and you know what, li'l one? You were so right. He was just like all the others, only his hard-on wouldn't go down, knowing I was just up the street. Which was forgiv-able, along with his dorky 'do and dry-cleaned jeans. But what wasn't was his love for blond, blue-eyed Toby Gleason in the fifth grade. I had a crush on him, believe it or not, and he passed me over for her whenever it was time to pick a partner for square dancing. Now it's 1976 and Toby Gleason is *Tubby* Gleason, the biggest, fattest Petunia this side of the Beltway. If she brought in her panties to Bean Cleaners, they'd be rich as Rockefeller. Now I toyed with the idea of stringing him along and dumping him at the altar, but I decided to spare his local-yokel ass. After all, he has to live out his miserable exis-tence with some homegrown Petunia. That's punishment enough!"

When we got to Glover, she picked up speed, driving mania-cally without stopping at red lights, stop signs, pedestrians.

"Not a day goes by that I don't run into that punk on his scooter and today I'm running *over* him," she warned the world.

"No, Cleo. Let's go home," I urged her.

She ignored me, still smoking.

"The fish is starting to stink up your car," I said out of desperation.

"Then hold your nose, because we're not going home!"

We drove around endlessly, with me begging her to stop. I was hysterical, but sedate compared with her.

"There he is!" she shouted.

Frog was loitering at the 7-Eleven, doing nothing. Cleo honked.

"Hey, Frog!"

He looked up. Mortal fear clouded his face. He pleaded, "Marcy! I need to talk to you!"

"Marcy doesn't talk to homely hicks anymore!" Cleo cut in. "Now hop on your tin can before I flatten it like one!"

Frog hopped on his moped and tore off out of the parking lot. Cleo was on his tail, yelling, "Let's do the bump, baby!"

"Cleo, don't do this," I was crying. "Let's go home! Please, Cleo, let's go home now!"

"Shut up!" she roared back, chasing Frog through intersections, strip centers, main roads, side streets.

And the darkness in Cleo was born, yelling as loud as the sky was high: "I'm going to run over you like an old brown shoe!

"I'm going to put you in a pauper's grave!

"I'm going to leave you for the vultures to feast on the grease under your fingernails!"

Cleo could have crushed him at any point, but that was not her plan, to have any rush-hour witnesses. What she wanted to do—and what she did—was maneuver him into a now-deserted industrial park. She taunted him with unspeakable insults as she ran him off the road and into a ditch so deep the bottom was not visible from where I sat.

Her last words were "Party hearty in hell, jackass hole!"

MY MIND went blank and the next thing I knew we were back on the Beltway. Cleo took the curves with liberated ease. Destination: Taco Town.

"That was fun," she declared.

"Cleo, do you think he's okay?"

"Do you honestly give a shit?"

"But we just left him there," I said.

"And he just violated you."

"I know, but…"

"But what? You want to bring him a bucket of fried chicken? How about a color TV?"

"No."

"Look, li'l one, he's just a common piece of trash who deserves to die in a ditch." Cleo said it so casually it scared me. "Believe me, the world will be a sweeter-smelling place without him."

WE TOOK our food and parked in our old spot. There Cleo devoured her beef 'n' bean burrito with masterful pleasure. Revenge had never tasted so good. I could not eat. My mind was stuck in that ditch.

"We are Kisook and Misook Moon, li'l one." She lovingly licked her fingers. "No one sees us as American, so why should we pretend to be? I am Kisook Moon from now on. Not Cleopatra, not Cleo. Kisook. And you're not Marcy anymore. Don't you see? You never were! You're Misook Moon. Just look in the mirror and match the name to the face."

"I like being Marcy," I stated.

"Marcy is the girl who was finger-fucked by a fuckhead named Frog. You don't want to be her anymore, do you?"

I fought tears and squeaked, "No."

"I'm just telling you like it is. Our identities are mixed up. Like Mom's English, like alphabet soup. Like those Simple Simon brothers. We may see ourselves one way but the rest of the world sees us another. We open our mouths and theirs drop— no *ah-so* accents! Racism is everywhere, it's in every home and garden you're *not* invited into. Sometimes it's better and easier to reinvent ourselves. As Misook Moon, you can forget Frog ever touched you. It never happened."

"Cleo—"

"Kisook," she corrected me.

"What's wrong with Dad?"

She lit up a cigarette and took the longest puff in history.

"It's like this, li'l one. You can dig out of poverty by studying hard and being number one in your class, you can travel the world and build highways and airports, you can materialize your dream of a house with shutters in the suburbs, but the only place you'll dig up peace of mind is in your own head."

.   .   .

I WONDERED about Frog all night, wondered where he was, back with his brothers or still in the ditch. Either way, he was calling me every slur known to hicks. I didn't wonder about him out of love or hate—I was too numb for such things. I wondered because I was afraid he was dead. Or not.

SINGING WITH my mother I could manage, but not conversation. I walked around shell-shocked. Everything was revolving in a wrong, warped direction. Everyone was moving away from me. My father was falling, my mother was singing. And then there was Cleo.

I had idolized her from the moment I opened my eyes, it seemed. What I always took for cool aloofness redefined itself as this: Cleo's darkness, unleashed. It was so dark the horror of it hadn't quite hit me yet. But I knew her darkness was there, living and breathing, ready to pounce. Like her flamboyantly winged eyeliner, it accented who she truly was. If questioned, she would say she was just defending her li'l sister's honor. Lie! Cleo never brought up the incident again, or asked me how I was coping.

THE MORNING of my father's arrival, I threw out my Satisfaction sandals and slipped on my moccasins, those old faithfuls. I scrubbed my lips good, just in case any trace of Berry Cherry remained. I was hoping the girl who had bade her father good-bye at the airport six weeks earlier would show up but she didn't. Too much had happened. My globe was turning too fast.

WE DROVE to Dulles Airport in the Torino—my mother, Cleo, and I—putting on our brave faces. The song had flown out of my mother's face and worry had flown in. Cleo was the stoic chauffeur. Not a word. I felt for the tiny box of Sunmaid raisins in my pocket. Would he take them from me and stare at the box like a little boy? Would faith and hope shine down on his unshaven, shriveled face? When I saw him walking out of the terminal in his favorite Hawaiian shirt, blue with lilac orchids, my eyes began to water.

"*Aigoo!*" my mother cried.

Amazingly, he looked tanned, sporty; as if he had never been sick a day in his life. The crowd always towered over him, but even when he was dressed in casual clothes, his proud stance dwarfed everyone. He strode toward us, a man in love. He took us all in his arms.

Who would have ever guessed?

"Dad," I squealed.

"Marcy, I thought perhaps you had a hippie hairdo now, or had grown six inches. In your letters, you sound like a changing girl. But you know something?"

"What?"

"You look the same."

"I do?"

"Yah."

I squeezed him so hard he had to gently prod me away.

"It's okay, Marcy. I am home now," he said in that familiar, low whisper of soap and Old Spice. This time I smelled something else, something like stale airplane air. "Tonight we go on a long walk, twice around. I ate a fattening meal on the airplane. Prime rib with potato and sour cream and oily gravy. How could I resist?"

I gave him the box of Sunmaid raisins. He blinked, at first confused. Then he understood and put it in his pocket without a word.

MY FATHER took over the wheel for the ride home. The family was tentatively quiet. Then he began to hum "Why Am I Always Waiting?" and our hearts settled back into place.

We thought he was safe in our arms. We were wrong.

IN THE days that followed, no one spoke of my father's nervous breakdown. On more than one occasion I heard him and Cleo behind closed doors. And though they would emerge spiritually spent and sweating with prayer, I now doubted Cleo possessed the power to heal him or anyone.

ON A night when I couldn't sleep, my father knocked on my bedroom door.

"Come in," I said.

His figure hovered over me. In the dark, he seemed only half here. Was I dreaming?

"Dad?"

"Yah?"

"Are you really okay?"

"I am in my beautiful home with my three beautiful girls. I am super okay. Don't worry about your old man. His ups and downs are a thing of the past. The more important question is, are you okay, Marcy?"

"Yes," I lied.

"Good, because I know you are at a very emotional age."

"An age of distraction," I reminded him.

"Yah."

"Dad"—I paused—"why do you have to take all those pills?"

"To regulate my blood pressure, you know that. I prefer not to take them, but that's the doctor's orders."

"You trust the doctor?"

"Why should I not? He is not a criminal."

"Meg's father doesn't have to take any pills."

"Maybe if he took a pill now and again, his blood would settle down and he would quit moving back and forth all over the place. One day Virginia, the next day Texas. Where next? The North Pole?"

We laughed.

If I didn't know any better, I could believe that my globe flicked on by itself. Like magic.

"Come here, Marcy. Let me show you all the places I visited on my mission."

We sat side by side, sharing my small chair. He began to re-trace his steps on my globe. His breath on my cheek was warm and harmonic. A story unfolded behind each city, town, hovel. A girl in rags selling flowers outside the palatial Erawan Hotel. A homeless artist who drew his caricature at Heathrow Airport. No mention of a hospital in Hong Kong or why his mission was cut short.

"Someday when I am an old man, you and I will take a trip together. Not just an ordinary trip but a trip to all four corners of the world. I promise I will be a feeble pain in the neck. You will have to lead me around. How I will enjoy that! To travel with my world-famous daughter. We will end up in Maui, where we had a good vacation, remember, right on Napili Bay? You insisted you wanted a Coppertone tan to look like a native girl and then you burnt to a crisp! And do you remember when we ordered pizza from that peculiar hippie waiter and he dropped it on a fat lady?"

In what city did his brain go topsy-turvy? Over what part of the South China Sea did he almost fall? I wanted him to point out these places but I was too afraid to ask. Then, while he was still talking about our Maui vacation, a theory came to me.

Maybe my father just didn't want to go to Korea—the last stop of his mission—to see his parents. Maybe he would rather jump off the plane than meet that destination. Could I blame him?

AFTER ALL her talk, Cleo was going back to college. Her Cleopatra eyeliner was gone now and she hustled around in a pair of baggy khakis, stuffing her clothes into a giant laundry bag. I watched.

"Are you going to be okay?" she asked me.

"Yes," I lied.

"I left half my wardrobe in the closet. Now that I'm Kisook Moon, silk and sequins don't fit me anymore. Take what you want."

"I don't want anything."

She hugged me. "Good girl, Misook."

"Why are you going back?" I asked her point-blank. "I thought you were dropping out."

She shrugged her cowardly shoulders. "I couldn't break the news to them in their condition. Dad's singing in the shower but choking to death inside. Mom's playing the piano just to keep him alive."

What about me? Didn't I count?

"So it's back to the pigpen dorm where Petunias snort in their sleep," she continued. "I love you, li'l one, but I can't watch this anymore. One more rock of emotion and this house is Popsicle sticks. I've got to split."

Split she did; in essence, forever.

AT LAST, Meg came home. I took her hand and pulled her under water and told her everything. When we came up for air, we were crying like babies.

.   .   .

M E G   H A D   brought back a bottle of something called Earth's Oil, God's Beauty Treatment.

"All the *gals* in Texas use it, and they have the creamiest complexions."

Quoting Cleo, I quipped, "They all have rawhide skin."

"No, they don't. Just the ones over thirty."

We were in the same upstairs bathroom as before. Light flooded the hallway as if it had never left. But nothing else was the same. This I knew the moment Meg stood over me. Her shag had grown out carelessly and her blue eyes, now fringed with black mascara, seemed smaller, almost blank.

"What's the matter, Meg?"

"Everything. All your crummy news and my brother's divorce. And my grades fell to hell in Texas. I had to take two courses over in summer school just so they wouldn't flunk me."

"But you never said anything on the phone."

"What was I supposed to say? 'Oh, hi, Marcy, remember me, the flunkee'?"

"Stop it. You're home now. We'll study together every day."

"You promise?"

"Yes."

"So I shouldn't worry?"

"No."

Our eyes met. Our faces were so close our breaths mingled. Her lips parted tragically.

"Marcy, are you going to be okay?"

"I don't know."

That was Meg's cue. She poured several golden drops of Earth's Oil onto her palm. She took a deep breath before rubbing her palms together and calling on all her powers, all her prayers, every positive spark missing from the day. I sat, not moving, not talking. She proceeded to rub the oil onto my forehead.

This time I could not feel her hands, her touch.

"I can't feel anything, Meg."

But Meg kept rubbing and repeating these words with hypnotic conviction: "You're going to be okay, Marcy. Forget about Frog. Forget about everything."

MEANWHILE, MY parents were living it up, going out for ice-cream and Red Lobster dinners. On Labor Day they went to a Korean picnic in a sprawling park on the Potomac waterfront in Alexandria where they played badminton and barbecued delicacies. What happened in Hong Kong was a plane disappearing into clouds.

And then, out of the blue, they announced they were going on a second honeymoon in Hawaii the next month. I was to stay at Meg's.

"Seven days in paradise," my father announced contentedly over a supper of sizzling *bulgogi*. "Sorry you cannot go with us, Marcy, but school comes first."

School? I hated school. I walked the hallways so stoned-looking everyone thought I was drugged out. Frog Fitzgerald? He was sorry he survived. My footsteps in the hallway sent him flying up and down staircases, into crowds.

"Mommy looks nice in her new muumuu she bought from the Spiegel catalogue, doesn't she?" my father asked.

"I don't understand why you have to go on a second honeymoon," I said.

"Marcy, Mommy and I married during the Korean War. We never went on a real honeymoon," he explained.

"No honeymoon," my mother agreed.

"Instead of violins we heard bombs in our ears," he added.

"Bombs!" my mother echoed.

"So?" I said.

"So even old fogies like to have fun. Besides, I am not too far from retirement age. I should like to thoroughly investigate the University of Hawaii campus. Maybe I will teach there."

"Farm orchid," my mother reminded him.

"Yah, I would like to visit an orchid farm, too. Grow things of beauty—*objets d'art*—in my retirement. Doesn't that sound like an idyllic life?"

"You're not retiring until you're sixty-five, Dad," I said. "That's twelve years from now."

"That may be true, but I don't want to wake up in twelve years and find I have nothing better to do than sleep on the sofa. Life has no structure, no meaning without a plan. Without my plan, Thailand would not have a highway to help the farmers get food from one destination to another. Without my plan, we could not afford to eat this delicious *bulgogi* Mommy has prepared. We might be dining on crackers instead. You must always have a plan for tomorrow. Even if nothing goes according

to plan, there is always its flame to return to, to guide you in another direction. Besides, Mommy and I want to eat sweet bean
buns at Ala Moana Mall."

"Twice as big as ones in Chinatown," she said. "Better taste!"

And they were off.

M EG A N D I were doing homework on her bed when her
parents knocked on the door. Before they even entered, I saw
shadows fly up on the ceiling. The whole room went gothic.
They crept in.

"Marcy."

We put down our pencils.

"Sweetheart, we have some bad news."

Meg grabbed my arm; papers flew off the bed.

Like monks, they crept closer. Death chanted in my ears.

Mr. Campbell spoke solemnly. "Your father suffered a stroke
in Honolulu."

"A stroke?" I said.

"We're so sorry, Marcy. He passed away in his sleep last
night."

A N D T H E N everything changed. What was once a tie-dyed
sky was a blackout forever. My father was gone and all the
cherished glory moments with Cleo, her shadow to bask in,
were gone, too.

Why we do the things we do is the eternal human question

with no answer. I stayed with my mother even though there were times when I felt I was the last person on earth she wanted to be with. My Korean face was not good enough for her—she needed the Korean soul to go with it. And yet I clung to her; she was the closest thing I had to my father. And for years I held on to the agonizing hope that Cleo would come home. She never did. My education ended long before I graduated from high school with this sorry lesson in life: Everyone—even those who say "I love you"—is a footstep from walking away forever.

19

A PERFECT DAY heats up White Sky. From the front porch of Cactus Bear, the desert lies beyond me in dreamy shades of adobe, and in my heart, smoke and feathers abound. How I love it here. I'm ready to walk in my moccasins that Pablo brushed and lovingly set out for me. Because of that small act—which he does every morning—I know I will be with him forever.

Once a mirage, now here, the Moccathon has arrived. The reality overwhelms me with goose bumps. A thousand times, while falling asleep, I have tried to envision this day. Me, here, with my canteen in tow.

Moccathoners gather on the mesa beyond.

"Luke, the Moccathon won't wait for slowpokes," I call out.

Luke is running late. It is the most natural thing in the world, to oversleep in White Sky, where dreams are deep and a coyote's howl leads you even deeper, so deep you don't ever want to come back. But Moccathons don't take place every day and Pablo's stone-ground wheat pancakes can wait.

"Luke!" I yell.

HE FINALLY stumbles out, followed by Pablo and June Moon. The sight of Luke in his rain-dance moccasins sets my heart in motion for this day.

We head out, waving goodbye.

Pablo waves back. "Hey, good luck, you two." He's got June Moon wrapped in a shawl, dreaming of a life out of reach.

EXPRESSION EASED Luke's mind. He spilled his guts, he bled, now he sleeps in and eats up a storm. But at heart he's still a glum boy, only halfway to healing. The rest of the way he has to go on his own.

While I'm introducing Luke to some other Moccathoners— Manny, Rebecca, and Ben, who also happen to be Pablo's friends from his bird-watching club, Birds 'R' Us—a drumroll takes over.

The Moccathon has officially begun.

DWARFING US and the desert plain, an archipelago of mountains reminds me that we can only walk so far. Perfect; I'll climb that mountain when I get to it. And while I'm climbing I'll listen to the language of the bristlecone pines, trees almost as old as God.

.   .   .

"TAKE A deep breath, Luke," I say. "Take it all in. High noon in the desert. The Nevada heat. The sky moving while we walk. The silvery-green tint of sage. I'm telling you, you may never experience a moment like this again."

"Okay," he says, looking out. But his eyes do not glitter.

"White Sky is unearthed before you like an ancient treasure trove and all you can say is *okay*?"

He shrugs.

"Talk to me, Luke. You played Expression and that's a first step. A good step. But your moccasins have a lot of walking and you've still got some talking to do."

Moccathoners mill all around us but the path we pave is private. Out of the blue, Luke says, "Are you going to tell my mom what I told you?"

"It's none of my business. I'm just glad you got it off your chest," I say.

Luke sighs, so relieved. "She'd go into shock if she knew. She had Stu figured for a god."

"Maybe he was in some ways, just not in all ways. Don't draw a single conclusion about someone based on one mistake. He had his good points, didn't he?"

"He spent a lot of time with me, even though he was real busy," Luke remembers.

"There you go. I'm sure he felt horrible about what happened."

"Then why'd he keep seeing her? Why didn't he just stop like he said he would?"

"Nobody's perfect, Luke. Everybody's human. Good people

sometimes do the wrong thing. But keep this in mind: You had nothing to do with Stu's death. Now, forgive him and move on. Right away."

We move on, in no hurry. We take it so slow the desert seems a still-life. The mountains, the sand, the cloudless sky. When Moccathoners breeze by us, the fragrance of sage stirs something in Luke.

"You won't tell her, will you?" he asks me again.

"Absolutely not."

Luke finally makes eye contact with me and I grab it for all it's worth.

"Cactus Bear," he says with a smile.

With that, we pick up speed, and something else, something much, much greater: a bond between us that not even distance or death can break. Maybe it's just me imagining things, but let me bask in this mirage of Luke and me. Oath: I will be here for him forever.

A N   H O U R later my legs are lead. I drank all my water, and now my canteen is dead weight. Meanwhile Luke is energized with humor while I'm wheezing.

"Marcy, it doesn't look like you're going to make it."

"Of course I am."

"Should I get you a wheelchair?"

"I'll keep walking even if my feet wear off into stumps. When I'm done—if I'm ever done—there won't be a suffering echo in White Sky."

"*Okay, okay, okay,*" Luke says.

.   .   .

ANOTHER HOUR later I've triumphed over that hump of
fatigue. In fact I'm loving every bleeding blister because every
bleeding blister means I'm closer to my horizon in heaven. And
in theory, when I'm at that elusive finish line, wherever it may
be, all of White Sky will be saved. With each step, I murmur,
"Cactus Bear."

I dig silence but the sound of Luke talking about the Internet under the Nevada sun is music to my ears.

"If you were hooked up, you could interact with all kinds of
people. Go into chat rooms and shoot the breeze with, you
know, other vegetarians or whoever. You wouldn't have to be so
isolated out here," he explains.

"I love the isolation, Luke. So vast with spirit. I can look out
and not see a living soul. Besides, when I want to chat, there's
always Pablo."

"Don't you guys ever get lonely?"

"Nope."

"But it's so quiet," he notes.

"That's what's so great. The silence."

He nods, trying with his whole heart to understand. Now that
his guard is down, he opens up to the sky and falls into a spell.

Then.

A rude awakening.

Rumbling behind us.

Not the awe-inspiring rumble of rain clouds in the desert,
but the ugly rumble of an automobile.

Luke falls out of his spell. We turn around.

Damn all the devils who dance around her! It's Cleo, maneuvering a Jeep. The Hollywood sunglasses and white wide-rimmed hat say it with a splash: The Global Gourmet Food Show was a success.

"Mom!" Luke cries.

"Luke!" she cries back.

"So how did it go?"

"What can I say? Mom was a hit on Broadway!"

"Cool, but I can't stop now." Luke grins goodbye. "I've got a long way to go."

"Just be through by four o'clock. We've got a plane to catch," Cleo calls after him.

LUKE IS so far ahead of me he's not even in my field of vision. Cleo paces me with a glare, as if I'm the one who's fallen under suspicion.

"Congratulations, you did your job," she says. "Luke has exited cyberspace. My hat's off to you. You're a psychotic quack with a knack. After curing those two dunces, I guess Luke was a breeze."

"I didn't cure them. Their father fired me and I left them dangling in their dyslexic fogs."

Cleo dismisses this with angry spit. "How could you pull a stunt like this? What's here besides sand and empty space?"

"And what's back in San Francisco? Big deal, a bay in the backyard."

"To people of sound minds, it's a very big deal. Do you have any idea how valuable our property is?"

"No, and I don't care. I do know that Luke had to take a bus all the way to White Sky to smile. And I do know that June Moon had to come here to get a good night's sleep. What price would you put on that?"

"I stopped by your shop first and saw her," she admits. "She did look quite peaceful with Pablo. By the way, why did you make him out to be some one-eyed ogre?"

"I didn't."

"He's gorgeous."

"I guess."

"You made him sound like he had an eyeball hanging out of its socket!" she insists.

"He's blind in one eye, that's all I said."

"Obviously the one he sees you with," she mutters meanly.

"You know, Cleo, I've dreamed of this Moccathon more times than you could imagine and not once were you ever in the picture."

"Did you picture yourself looking like a cripple who lost her crutches? My God, couldn't you afford a pair of walking shoes?"

"It's called a Moccathon, Cleo. A Moccathon."

But she's got a point. I'm dragging, so thirsty I'm croaking up dust. In need of crutches, water, White Sky magic. Cleo the vulturess stalks me.

"Marcy, what's going on here?"

"Life in living color, Cleo. Take it in, if you've got the guts."

"What's that supposed to mean?"

"That you're not worthy of your children. Your heart is a cracked, black, loveless thing."

"I don't believe this. I suppose you've been feeding Luke this garbage, along with your shitty soup. Trash me some more while you're at it."

"You're dangerous. That's why I took them."

"Where's the local loony bin? You've been out in this dust bowl too long. Your brain's tumbleweed. What do you mean, dangerous? How could you think I could hurt anyone?"

"You hurt Frog Fitzgerald."

"Who?"

"Yes, drove him into a ditch and left him to rot."

"Who the hell is Frog Fitzgerald?"

"Think back. To the summer you were Cleopatra Moon."

"Cleopatra Moon?" She blinks behind her sunglasses until it all comes back to her. "Are you talking about that miserable little hick? Sure, I drove him into a ditch. I knew it wasn't deep— I used to make out and more down there. But you're damn right I didn't care. Why should I? He took advantage of you and you were my baby sister. Why am I the villain here? You should be mad at him, not me. I did it for you!"

"Cleopatra Moon, you were pissed off at the world and you did it for you!"

"You're the one who's pissed off at the world. So pissed off you have to hide out here in sand land. You act like I ruined your life!"

"You did ruin my life!"

"What? What did I ever do to you?"

I never thought I would say these words. I thought I would die first. But somehow the words leave my lips without punch, without sarcasm.

"Cleo, you left me to rot, too. You made a life without me while I took care of a mother who never cared for my company in the first place."

A long pause later, she utters a sick "Oh."

For the first time in many years we are moving in sync; so slowly we're almost going backwards. I ask her the question I've been damning her for, for so many years: "Why didn't you ever come back after Dad died?"

Cleo looks up, then down, with achy, suicidal agony. She closes her eyes, wishing this would all go away until she remembers she's at the wheel. Finally, she takes a deep breath and says, "I guess a part of me felt like if I wasn't home, I could almost make believe he was still alive. Off on a mission or in the back yard, watering that dogwood tree that would never blossom. Then too much time passed, too much had changed; it was just too late to come home. I didn't know how to be part of the family anymore. Without Dad. God, it's been so long since I've said that. *Dad.* I couldn't, I still can't, accept his death. Believe it or not—and I know you won't—I loved him too much. Yes, I left you and Mom and I'm sorry. But I was just a kid myself."

"And I was fourteen, Cleo. You were God and my big sister all wrapped up in one. You could part the water and sky and the Beltway traffic."

She's thoroughly stunned. "Me? God?"

"And you left me to handle all of Mom's affairs. You knew she would never go to anyone for help. There I was, too young to drive, figuring out her inheritance taxes."

Cleo squints. "But you were the genius. You could do all that blindfolded."

"No, I *became* blindfolded. My life ended up being nothing but Mom and her bottomless well of grief!"

"I'm sorry, Marcy. I really am."

"Oh, sure, I was the genius. I never even made it to college!"

"Why not? Who stopped you?"

"My own mind stopped me. I had spun off the globe. And I didn't know how to get back on."

"I'm sorry," she repeats.

"When she chose the Hanguk Home over me, I had nobody, Cleo. Nobody."

"Marcy, I said I'm sorry!"

I can't help myself; I want to make her even sorrier. Stu's infidelity—her motivation for murder—in the wide-open sky would do the trick. I promised Luke I wouldn't, but it was Cleo who had called this my big moment. And an eye for an eye, Pablo had said. Besides, we're talking about decades of pent-up pain. This, I deserve.

"Cleo, I know the truth about Stu."

Curiosity dawns on her face. "What?"

Hold on for one hallucinating minute. I may be delirious but her Little Miss Innocent act isn't going to work on me. I know the truth about Stu and I know the darkness in Cleo. Come out, come out, wherever you are, and admit your dirty deed.

"Marcy, what did you know about him? Tell me."

God, oh God, oh God, I can't think, see, or sweat straight. God, oh God, oh God, why isn't she acting guilty? Like a giant sandstorm in my face, it hits me: Cleo may never be Mother of the Year, but she didn't murder Stu. It's as plain as the naïve

look on her face. That was me, wishing it was so. Even the
Other Woman went right by her.

The fantasy to hurt Cleo fades like a dream. Why tell her,
why hurt her, just because she hurt me? To her, my pain is as
distant as the stars on a sun-washed summer day. There was a
time Cleo was my God and parted the Beltway traffic but never
the water or the sky. That was me, dreaming it was so.

Like the psychotic quack she accused me of being, I say, "I
know he loved you and the kids."

"Yes, he did," she says, canvassing me for signs of heat stroke.
"Stu was a fine father and husband. The best. We were soul
mates from the word go. We belonged to our own exclusive
club: Each Other. I marinated the meat, he grilled it, and it all
went down deliciously." She clutches her heart, feels for him,
his memory, something, anything. Then her sky falls. "My God,
my husband is dead. The Global Gourmet Food Show is over
and my husband is dead," she says, slowing down to a stop,
then slipping into prayer.

Her ceremony is private, her downcast hat shuns me. I cannot read lips but the spirits tell me she is praying belatedly for
the two dead men in her life.

On I crawl like some deformed desert crab. Too soon, Cleo's
coasting along with me, revived with prayer.

"Marcy, get in! It's a thousand degrees out here!"

"No, I can't stop now."

"Look, I'll sponsor Luke, too. Just stop before you kill yourself. You look sick. Dangerously sick."

"No, I need to walk forever."

"I'll name a sauce after you. Marcy's Marvelous Soup Sauce!

I'll donate fifty percent of its profits to Cactus Bear. Just stop walking, damn it, and get in the car. I don't want you to die out here in the desert like a scene from some B movie."

"You don't understand," I say, starting to feel faint. "If I don't finish the Moccathon..."

"What, Marcy? What will happen if you don't finish?"

I'm too out of breath to speak; my throat is scorched sand. Where is my vision? Where is Cactus Bear? Is it like the original? Lost, stolen, gone. My eternal walk is going nowhere.

"I have to help him," I say.

"Who? Who do you have to help, Marcy?"

I search my sad, exhausted soul for an answer.

"Oh...my...God," Cleo says, probing me. "You think Dad's over there, don't you?"

"Dad?"

"Yes, yes, yes! Marcy, don't you see? You've built up this Moccathon in your mind as some kind of pilgrimage to some meeting ground, yes, some sacred meeting ground, for you and Dad. That's what all this is ultimately all about." She is wholly triumphant. "Do you remember how you and Dad used to take walks together? Only you could never keep up with him. Now you're hoping to catch up to him, walk right out of this life into another. I'm sure you want to save those Indians; you've always had a thing for underdogs. But this is about saving Dad, too. I don't want to sound mean, Marcy, but it's too late. Now get in the car or my offer drops to forty percent. We're talking mega money here, not chump change."

I'm on my last leg, my last gasp. "He needed my help. But I couldn't help him."

"He needed spiritual salvation. Neither of us could give him that. But you were the daughter of his dreams. What more do you want? Now, look, my final offer is thirty percent or else nothing and I'm driving away. Get in the Jeep or die a fool!"

Cleo was too drunk, high, hospitalized, fucked-up at the time to remember that I was not the daughter of his dreams that final summer of his life. And what about today? Could he have dreamed up this pathetic scene? My Moccathon is over. Nothing miraculous happened.

Until now.

Yes.

I hear it coming.

Thunder rolling in.

It rolls over the Great Basin and leaves me shivering.

"Luke's moccasins," I whisper.

"What did you say?" Cleo says.

"Luke's rain-dance moccasins!" I shout.

"And that means?"

"It means the rain is talking to me. It's saying the White Sky spirits are happy. Luke and I did good—now the White Sky won't go extinct. Their magic will return! The rain is hurrahing *Cactus Bear!* for Luke, too. He walked and walked and walked and he's still walking!"

"Talking rain? White Sky spirits? Cactus Bear? What are you..."

Rain dances over us. I stand with my face to the sky, drinking rain, magic rain, and listen to its enchanted monologue. And on its highest plane it is communicating this to me: *Marcy's Marvelous Soup Sauce. Mega Money for the White Sky Tribe.* Cleo's lips are moving but she's a silent movie. The rain, the revelation, the release is drowning her out. What comes through is a voice from the past and a signature honk—*beep, beep, beeeep!*—all calling up something I could never imagine again until today. My big sister at the wheel.

"Hop in, li'l one!"

And I do.

WE SETTLE down to supper. Pablo has prepared a special meal tonight. Wild rice with acorn squash. Pasta with roasted bell peppers. Muffins with chives snipped from his pot on the windowsill. He was cooking and cleaning and kissing June Moon at the same time, knowing he would feed on this dream when everyone was gone.

Our table is set à la Cactus Bear. Nothing matches. Each plate, each bowl, each cracked cup—like each person at the table—has a story to tell.

"So I hear you're in the sauce business, Cleo." Pablo pours a round of sassafras tea. "Sounds very lucrative."

"So far. But I have to keep my wits about me. In business, the wind blows and you've got to blow with it. Tastes change. What's hot today is history tomorrow."

"Beware of cold calls from junior brokers," he warns her. "These guys go through Dun and Bradstreet looking for suckers."

"Which I'm not," Cleo says, savoring every bite.

"Timing is the key. You have to know when to expand and when to stop."

"That's the master key," she agrees.

"You know," Pablo says, "in my cooking class we learned how to prepare some basic sauces, nothing gourmet, though."

"Who needs sauce when you cook like this? Pablo, you're truly gifted," she says.

"Why, thank you, Cleo."

"I'm glad you decided to stay on through the weekend," I chime in.

"Ditto," Pablo punctuates.

"Double ditto," Luke says.

"After all, *rush* is a four-letter word in White Sky," I say.

"Did I have a choice? Luke isn't budging until—How did you put it?" Cleo asks him drowsily, a mother in love.

"Until your bones settle your soul down," he expertly coins.

"Until my bones settle my soul down." Cleo chews on this concept while she reaches for the basket of muffins.

"And we're not leaving until we get Marcy a computer," Luke says.

"Hey, hey," I say, "who said anything about a computer?"

"Lighten up, it's not like it's a four-letter word," Luke says. "You've got to get hooked up. You and Mom are kind of like partners now. You need to know what's going on in the real world. Not that your world isn't real, too. Moccasins are cool. But so is money. And Marcy's Marvelous Soup Sauce is super cool."

"I'm cool with that," I concede. "Especially since your mom generously reconsidered her initial offer."

"Speaking of money"—Cleo clears her throat—"I understand you were a major number cruncher in L.A., Pablo. Any hope of getting you back into it? I need someone. You could do it from here, of course."

"Sorry, the only numbers I crunch are here at Cactus Bear. But hey, thanks for the offer," Pablo says.

Below, the chimes sound; Pablo excuses himself.

"Luke, I was wondering about something," I begin.

"Yeah?"

"Now that you've walked the earth in rain-dance moccasins and seen mirages of water so blue you swam in them, now that you've touched the sky with your unearthed soul and have been rained on by White Sky spirits, now that you've promised to come visit us at least four times a year..."

"Yeah?"

"Can I have my globe back?"

AFTERWARD, PABLO and I watch the desert sun go down from our front porch swing. We swing in dreamlike harmony.

"Who was at the door earlier?" I ask.

"No one," Pablo says.

Inside, Luke is showing Cleo our moccasin rack. Somehow this thought puts calm in my heart. Cleo, trying on moccasins.

"I plead temporary insanity," I tell Pablo. "I guess I was so angry she deserted me I lost sight of things."

"Anger can do that. Next stop, madness."

"No more anger," I say.

"Let it go."

"It's gone."

"By the way, Marcy, I'm going to tell you something and I

don't want you to question it, ever."

"What's that?"

"I love you and I will never leave you. Never."

"Not even if I hide all your herbs?"

"Well, I'll have to think about that."

We swing.

"Pablo?"

"Yes?"

"I wonder what my mother is doing right now."

Pablo holds me. "Having a ball in the Hanguk Home."

"Last I heard, she had sold more calendars in Koreatown than any other resident."

"Was there a prize?"

"A fifty-dollar certificate to the Hanguk Mall."

"Time to go shopping!"

"In the mood for meditation?" Pablo asks me.

"Yes, I'm ready to find the center of my soul."

We hold hands with newfound pleasure. A tingle ripples through us. We take deep, synchronized breaths until we are one. At the same instant we chant "Cactus Bear."

"Wow," Pablo says.

"Double wow," I say.

"Do you think we'll be too old for this someday?" Pablo wonders.

"Never," I say.

"I'm glad you forgave Cleo. Your soul is lighter now. I can feel it."

"I'm floating."

"Now that you've made peace with the past, it's time to move on to today. And today is our time. Yours and mine. It's time we get married and adopt a White Sky baby. No more brain strain. Just say yes."

"Whoa, there, Pablo," I say.

"Why?"

"Because I want to hear you say it again."

Pablo breaks into a smile and a song. *"Marcy Moon, now I'm no longer alone..."*

Cleo steps onto the porch wearing earth-tone moccasins and holding June Moon—both hers forever. Pablo witnesses this sight and sighs across the desert. Time is running out. He gets up and begs Cleo for the baby. Tonight June Moon is his. The two wander as one to the other side of the porch and into their own little world.

"May I have a seat?" Cleo asks me.

"Sure."

We swing as twilight falls over us. I am suddenly moved by everyone's presence around me and by all the faraway stars struggling to sparkle.

"Cleo, I'm so sorry I said all those rotten things."

She laughs. "I probably deserved some of them." Then: "Talking about Dad today brought back a million memories, Marcy. Remember all those postcards he wrote from overseas? One to each of us, just about every day. Do you know why he wrote so many?"

"Because he missed us."

"Yes, of course he missed us. But that's not why he dedicated every free minute of his time to writing us. It was because he was never sure of anyone's love for him. Not even ours. When we wrote back, he felt a little bit more assured. But that feeling never lasted."

"What could we have done, Cleo?"

"Two daughters can't fix a father's depression. Stuff like that starts so early. That's the killer, the sad part, the part we can't do anything about. But you know what?"

"What?"

"You've done miracles with my son."

LUKE POKES his head out the door. "Hey, Marcy, I just sold another magic stone. What's my commission?"

"An invitation to swing with your mom and me."

"Sorry," Luke says, disappearing back inside, "but I've got customers waiting."

Cleo and I swing for so long time seems like a mystery. Our thoughts scatter the stars and make them glow. We swing and we swing and we swing until we find ourselves spinning on the same globe. Again, the chimes sound. Our fingertips touch and a new flame is born.

My "Dream On" Essay
by Marcy Moon

When I'm with my big sister Cleo, time flies. We take off in her red Mustang and listen to tunes. We go shopping and swimming, too, but cruising around is much more fun. When the top's down, I feel as free as a bird, like no one will ever catch up with us.

When I'm with Cleo, all the lonely moments go away. Everything seems sunny and better than before. She takes me almost everywhere she goes and never makes me feel like a tagalong. She treats me to lunch and tells me I can order anything on the menu, not just the special. That's because I'm special, she says. Cleo is always saying nice things like that to me.

When I'm with Cleo, I see everyone staring at her. That's because she's so beautiful. She has the most beautiful long black hair and she wears the coolest clothes. But she's beautiful inside, too. I'm so proud that she's my sister.

When I'm with Cleo, I believe that someday we'll hang out together every day, not just when she's back from college. When she gets her own place, I'll spend all my time over there. We'll cover the walls with posters and listen to our favorite albums. We'll eat pepperoni pizza and talk about boys. We'll have lots of good times.

When I'm with Cleo, every minute is filled with magic.

I dream on that we will be sisters forever.

THE END